Prologue

January, 1962

I wake up and for a few moments, I feel okay, like maybe today is just another day. I stretch my arms out from under the covers and notice that the room is chilly. Goose pimples break out on my arms, now that they are bare. I've forgotten and left the window open again.

It's a perfectly normal window. It has frilly, white lace curtains I long ago stopped noticing. Even though it's an ordinary window, suddenly when I see it, I'm not happy anymore. Just like that. Just like being slapped. I remember last night and what a disaster it was.

Very soon, I'm going to have to choose between what I've always supposed I would have and what I never even knew I wanted. I've given half answers and no answers and actually told lies which I never imagined I'd do. I've made a mess of things for sure. All I want to do is throw the covers over my head and cry.

My name is Eleanor Wilson. I live in a big, fancy house, in a Connecticut suburb of New York City. The house seems too big for just the three of us. I care about my parents but if ever someone was deposited by an alien space craft into a life that didn't make sense for them, it was me.

My parents don't go to the picture shows but they never stopped me from going. I love the movies. A couple of summers ago, it seemed like every movie I saw with Paul or Rosemary or some friend from school, had an alien in it. The aliens were strange and scary. I always thought maybe we'd be strange and scary to them too although it never seemed that way in the movies. I didn't wonder what it would feel like to be one of those aliens. I already knew.

When I was six, I got into trouble for climbing trees with the gardener's kids. It would have been okay, if I hadn't fallen out and broken my arm. For my parents, the horror wasn't that their only daughter was hurt, No, the horror was having their only daughter climb trees with the gardener's kids in the first place.

When I was twelve, the trouble was with horses. Well-bred ladies of my age would ride horses and attend dressage competitions. They wore jodhpurs and immaculate riding hats. My parents hoped to cultivate ladylike habits in me though horsewoman-ship.

I like animals in general and I think horses are okay. Plus, hanging around at the stables, gave me an excuse not to have to wear a dress. I tolerate it now but I wasn't always so patient. Unfortunately, I wasn't all that interested in horsewoman-ship.

I was interested in what the breeder did when he brought the stallion from the stud farm. I was interested in what the farrier did when he shod the horses. I was really interested in what the vet did. I followed him around mercilessly and asked him endless questions. Why was he doing this or that? What sort of medicine could you use on an infection in a horse? Would that be different for a dog? Did house cats catch the flu? Had he ever treated a goldfish?

Finally, instead of losing all patience with me, he made me his assistant. While other girls, like Rosemary, were passionate about shoes and dresses, my proudest 12-year-old moment involved helping the vet deliver a breach foal. My parents were not happy. Again.

After that incident, surprisingly, the remainder of my teenage years were fairly calm. I could feel rebellion trying to surface in me and I would tamp it back down. I was trying to be the daughter my parents wanted. Surely, if I kept doing the things that were expected of me, I would eventually understand the benefits of those things wouldn't I? I've always been stubborn and I felt sure I could fix myself and meet my parent's standards through sheer force of will.

I'm eighteen now and aside from the aforementioned deviations, there had been only one truly contentious issues between my parents and I.

Granted, my one issue was a doozy, at least for my mother. Young ladies in my social circle "come out" to society. Their families host lavish parties, sometime for weeks leading up to a debutante's ball. My mother speaks fondly and frequently of her own debut. She talks for hours about the food, the dresses, the dancing. My father insists he was smitten utterly with her after that night.

But despite their misty-eyed nostalgia, despite their insistence on tradition, despite my real desire to conform myself to their world, I can't bring myself to become a debutante. My parents beg, cajole and hope although amazingly, they never outright insist and I never give in. The issues never completely goes away. It simmers under the surface mostly and every so often bubbles over. There are entreaties on both sides; calm and logical on their side and impassioned on mine. We are ever at an impasse.

I don't have illusions about my powers of persuasion. I'm reasonably certain that I've only been allowed to get away with the social anomaly is because of Paul.

Paul Philip Putnam III is handsome, polite and charming. He has never made a social miss step. Paul Philip Putnam the first drank brandy and discussed books with my grandfather. Paul Philip Putnam II is my father's law partner. Inexplicably, Paul Philip Putnam the third decided when he was twelve and I was eight that we would be married.

He's never formally asked me. I have no engagement ring, a fact which Rosemary regularly urges me to remedy by asking him for one. But I don't care. I know that Paul is not cheap or careless and when the time is right, surely I'll get one. Ring or not, no one has ever questioned that this would happen. Not Paul's parents. Not my parents. Not even me...until recently.

Anyway, since one of the points of a debut is to introduce a young lady to eligible young men, my parents were perhaps more willing to let it go. After all, I wouldn't have to meet anyone to marry since my marrying Paul was a forgone conclusion. I was pretty sure my mother felt she would be able to throw all of her party planning ambitions into engagement parties, bridal showers and a wedding.

A little more than six months ago, things started to go wrong. Or right. Or something.

⌘⌘⌘⌘⌘

June 1961

The week after high school graduation, I sat on Rosemary's bed, watching her try on dresses. Rosemary is Paul's younger sister. Unlike me, she's been dreaming of her debutante's ball since she could toddle.

Rosemary had been my best friend for years. Not only was she my best friend, she was my hero. Like her brother, she never missed a social cue. Not only did she not miss them, she understood why they were important. She liked etiquette. Where I was generally perplexed about why certain things had to be done and at what time, Rosemary loved the social rules. She was good at them. They made her feel safe.

Somewhere around junior high, I started to get excited about history, geography and other cultures. I became a voracious reader and I dreamed of traveling. Rosemary continued to love dresses, shoes and jewelry. I pulled away from her a little then. She was self-absorbed enough not to notice my deflection.

Rosemary's debut was coming up at the beginning of September.

"…and I was thinking of the blue chiffon for the barbeque with these gloves but which hat?"

"I'm sorry, what?" I had absolutely no idea what she'd been saying.

She gave me a quick hug. I was sweating just sitting there but her skin was cool to the touch.

"Poor Eleanor. You didn't get a debut. I must be making you awfully unhappy."

I smiled at her. Rosemary knew my lack of debutante status was my own choice but she couldn't quite wrap her brain around it. She couldn't imagine not wanting it, so she was sure I'd been denied somehow.

"That dress is lovely," I said.

Her face lit up. Rosemary could be shallow sometimes but she was never mean.

That week was filled with more dresses and shopping. By the end of the week, I was losing my mind. I knew the rest of my summer would follow the pattern of that first week. If I had to look at many more dresses, I felt sure I would collapse in a drooling, twitching heap.

Unlike lots of girls in my position, I would have been happy to work. My parents weren't in favor of my getting any sort of traditional job since they were sure I'd be marrying Paul soon and quitting anyway. Married women in my circle did not work.

Despite that, I'd actually had a babysitting job for the past three summers. The wife of a lawyer in my father's firm had decided she needed more time during the summers for her bridge club and lunch dates. She and her husband had a boy and a girl. Joe was five when I started to baby sit and Jen was three.

They were great kids. They weren't spoiled although I'm not sure I could say the same for their mother. She was accustomed to getting everything she wanted. Fortunately, I didn't have to deal with her too much. She was always running off somewhere and that's why she needed a babysitter.

I had a ton of fun with Joe and Jen. Babysitting didn't even seem like a job at all. Maybe I was just a kid at heart but I loved reading stories and coloring and playing games. Their family had moved away, the previous winter. I really missed them. I also missed the distraction that babysitting had provided. For three years, I had known what I was going to do with myself during the summer.

If I had my way, I'd have been getting ready to go off to college. I truly wanted to study anthropology or sociology or psychology or all of them. It wasn't going to happen though. My father and I had had the discussion a couple of years before, when I was still in high school.

It wasn't that my father was opposed to college for women but he hated extravagance. My parents had money and we lived very comfortably. Compared to other families in our social circle though, we lived modestly. Since it seemed inevitable that I would marry Paul, be well supported and probably never need to work, my father saw a college education for me, as an extravagance. I would be going, just to go. In my father's eyes, it served no purpose.

Surprisingly, it was Paul who presented a solution to my boredom. Paul and I have a standing Saturday dinner date at our parents' country club. I didn't want to complain specifically about Rosemary. After all, she was Paul's sister and my friend as well. Plus, my complaint wasn't specifically with her. It was really with too many dresses.

"So, I hear you've had a week of endless dresses," Paul said at dinner.

I couldn't tell if his tone was lightly teasing or if he was just stating a fact.

"Endless, is right," I said. I must have also rolled my eyes.

Paul raised an eyebrow quizzically.

"I love Rosemary," I quickly reassured him. "But I'm so bored. I like learning new things. I like books. Dresses aren't really my first love," I reminded him. "I guess, I miss school," I finished wistfully.

That really didn't sufficiently describe my frustration but it wasn't untrue either.

"You know that I don't want us to get married until I invest some additional time at the firm," he cautioned.

I'll give Paul this, he wasn't afraid to work hard. Our fathers owned the law firm where he was making his career but he never behaved like he was entitled to work there. I admired this about him. I suspected I would probably have a similar work ethic if I was ever able to actually work.

"I'm not suggesting that you need to entertain me," I said. I didn't say that I wasn't entirely convinced that marriage was going to relieve my sense of ennui anyway.

"Rosemary, my mother, your mother - they're all great at planning parties and organizing events. They know which clothes to wear and how to be gracious hostesses. All those things just don't make me as happy as they make them," I explained. I didn't say that not only did they not make me happy, I wasn't even all that good at them.

Paul patted my hand.

"Of course, someday you'll be great at all those things and they *will* make you happy."

Paul had been convinced for years that I would somehow grow into a passionate understanding of the social graces. I didn't tell him I seriously doubted that would happen. I was beginning to feel more stuck than ever, when Paul surprised me.

"Miss Cavendish in our office recently graduated from a secretarial school in the city. She speaks highly of her training and seems quite competent. Would you be interested in secretarial school, Eleanor?"

Secretarial school had never crossed my mind, even briefly.

When I daydreamed about my ideal life, those dreams had never included filing and shorthand, Then I thought about spending all day, every day, for the rest of the summer watching Rosemary trying on dresses.

"Oh, Paul," I gushed. "I would love secretarial school!"

"I think it runs for several months," he said questioningly.

Was I willing to commit several months to secretarial school? I thought of the rest of the summer and endless dresses. I thought of the months beyond, where my mother would undoubtedly badger me about my own lack of a debut. I didn't have to think very long.

"Several months would be fine," I said. "It'll keep me out of your hair while you work on your career," I added.

I wasn't needy. Paul and I both knew it but I felt it wouldn't hurt to put an element of benefit for him in there, even if it was unnecessary.

"I'll look into it for you," Paul said.

⌘⌘⌘⌘⌘

Paul knew I was disappointed about the whole college thing. Even my parents knew too, although they didn't plan to do anything to remedy my disappointment. What nobody knew, was that I had even bigger, more outlandish dreams for myself.

Back in the early spring, President Kennedy had announced the formation of a Peace Corps. We watched the announcement on TV. My father thought it would be good for young people to perform a service for less fortunate people elsewhere in the world.

Paul commented that he hoped the new volunteers would be better trained than their older foreign service counterparts. He had read somewhere that many of the people currently in foreign service barely even spoke the languages of the countries they served. My mother fretted over people contracting diseases. Rosemary pondered how volunteers would get their laundry clean.

I said nothing. Not because I had nothing to say but because the president's brief announcement left me dumbfounded. I wanted to join the Peace Corps. My reaction was immediate. I felt it was something I had to do. But how could I join the Peace Corps? I had no experience in engineering or irrigation or agriculture. I didn't speak a foreign language. I had no medical training. Aside from my notable lack of any valuable skills, my parents didn't even want me to go to college. How was I going to convince them I belonged in a foreign country?

A few weeks later, Rosemary and I went to the movies and there was a newsreel all about the Peace Corps. Grainy images of smiling people making bricks and building schools filled the screen. "These people are the forerunners of the newly formed Peace Corps," the narrator intoned. Again I had that peculiar sense of belonging. Of feeling like that was where I was supposed to be. It made absolutely no sense. When the theater held over the movie, I talked Rosemary into seeing it again.

"Gee," she said. "I had no idea you were so interested in the Absentminded Professor."

I didn't tell her it wasn't Fred McMurray who'd caught my attention but that five minute newsreel. I even went back one more time by myself. I never went to the movies alone but I had to see that newsreel again. I left before the movie started but I was sure this meant something transformational for me. I was enamored. I even loved the way President Kennedy had said "emerging nations" instead of third-world countries. It was respectful. It implied that volunteers would get as much as they gave. The president said volunteers would learn as much as they would teach. The announcer said it was "a bold challenge to positive action."

My longing for the Peace Corps was irrational and inexplicable. I couldn't even explain it to myself in my own mind. Until I could do that, I wouldn't be able to explain it to someone else. I knew I'd have to put it on hold temporarily and make do with secretarial school.

If I had suggested secretarial school, my parents would have thought it was a useless pursuit. Since Paul broached the topic, it was a good idea. Paul reminded my father that I was likely to get bored now that high school was over. He reminded my parents that my being bored might end with my being in trouble. There was certainly precedent for it. He implied that secretarial school might be a safe place for me temporarily. I'd comported myself very well to their standards aside from the no debut thing but no one had forgotten the broken arm or the vet.

Paul even offered to pay for my tuition. He handled my enrollment. As always, Paul was highly efficient and before I knew it I was about to begin secretarial school. If only he'd known that it would set off a whole chain of events which would spiral out of everyone's control.

⌘⌘⌘⌘⌘

"What is that?" my father demanded, as if it wasn't obvious.

"It's a 1949 Nash Airflyte," I said.

"I've been imprecise," my father allowed in what I liked to think of as his lawyerly voice.

"Allow me to re-phrase the question. To whom does it belong and why is it wheezing in our driveway?"

The elderly Nash spluttered in our circular driveway, despite the fact that I'd turned off the ignition and the keys dangled from my hand.

"I needed a car for secretarial school," I explained.

My father walked to his office every single day regardless of the weather. When he needed to go into the city, he hired a driver. A pristine Buick Roadmaster sat in our garage for times when we took family vacations or my parents went to dinner with friends.

"William can drive you," my father insisted. William was my father's sometime chauffeur.

I decided to appeal to his sense of importance. My father wasn't really arrogant but he was proud of the work he did.

"William can't be carting me back and forth every day. You may need him to take you somewhere. Your work is important, Daddy. I'm only going to secretarial school."

"If you must drive, you can take my car," he said.

"I would be so afraid of it getting scratched in the city," I said and it was true.

I had taken driver education in school with my classmates and had passed my license test without a problem. But my father kept the Buick in immaculate, like-new condition and driving it intimidated me.

My father eyed the Nash dubiously. In the past I would have asked my parents about buying a car. I would have asked Paul and probably taken him with me to the dealership. But in the few days since Paul had suggested secretarial school, the idea had really grown on me. I had attended elementary and high school with Rosemary and other kids from our same social group. I realized that in secretarial school, I'd be with a whole group of people who I didn't know and who didn't know me. The prospect was inherently exciting and it made me a little bit reckless.

I had gone to the dealership alone with my saved up babysitting money. I could have afforded a much better car than the old Nash with my father's or Paul's help but it was suddenly really important to me to do it myself. The Nash was a color somewhere between brown and mauve. Its seats folded down into twin beds. The dealer said they'd be ideal for camping, not that I was probably going to ever go camping. The car sputtered. It coughed. It rattled in ways I was sure might be dangerous or at least expensive. Yet I loved this car. It had been mine for less than an hour but it was all mine. I would fight for it.

Something of this must have showed in my face, for my father looked momentarily indecisive.

"I just want to get there myself, without bothering you or mother or Paul. And Paul thinks this could be a great opportunity for me," I couldn't resist adding.

I could see my father fight a brief internal battle with himself. He was clearly really unhappy with my purchase of this car. By the same token, I had made some valid points about needing it. He knew that boredom and I were probably not a good combination and that secretarial school was probably the best place for me at least temporarily. I had even suggested I might help out at his firm after graduating, so he knew he'd be able to keep an eye on me until Paul was finally ready to get married.

"Is it safe?" he asked, suspiciously eying the Nash again.

"Of course," I lied. I had no idea if the car was safe or not.

My father sighed heavily. "Keep it parked by the gatehouse," he said resignedly and walked away.

Our house was pretty old. The gatehouse had once been just that. When we'd been younger, I'd turned it into sort of a clubhouse. Paul would play there sometimes with me although he was already almost too old to care about it by the time I discovered it. Rosemary was always afraid of getting dirty there. I played there some with the gardener's kids although I didn't see as much of them after the arm-breaking incident.

Now the gatehouse housed some old toboggans and skates, some assorted rakes and potting soil and not much else. There was a small lane that led from the back of the house where my room was. It ran past the gatehouse and dumped out onto the main street. Long before I was born, when the house was new, the lane by the gatehouse had been the main entrance to the property. Then my grandfather had our current driveway built as a more direct way to the road. This parking spot would prove fortuitous for me in a couple of different ways.

⌘⌘⌘⌘⌘

The night before secretarial school began, I slept poorly. I tossed and turned, finally dozing off just as the sky was beginning to turn from black to indigo. I dreamed that I was in Africa, with the Peace Corps, building a hospital. In the dream, Paul had admonished me about going. He said I'd surely regret it. Yet in the dream I was happy. When the alarm went off a little while later, I was sorry the dream had ended. I felt that sense of happiness drain from me when I realized it hadn't been real. It was replaced with a more practical nervous optimism as I thought of secretarial school.

Secretarial school was held on the fifth floor of an ugly brick building about thirty minutes from my house. The first four floors were devoted to office space. The sixth and top floor held a cooking school. All kinds of wonderful smells would come wafting down from above.

The teacher for secretarial school was named Mrs. Rhineberg. She spoke in a heavily accented monotone. Her inflection was very odd. She paused in spots where she should have kept talking and rushed on in spots where she might have spoken more slowly. She said she had moved to America from Austria just before the war. I'd obviously never heard her speak prior to emigrating to the United States but I wasn't sure twenty years of practice had helped her much.

Mrs. Rhineberg spent most of the first class explaining exactly what we'd be learning. For my part, I would have preferred to just jump into the learning without all the explanation but clearly she had a plan and did not deviate from the plan.

Many of the women in the class were obviously from families and social situations similar to mine. A lot of them were around my age. They were bored socialites, killing time until they got married. They wore white gloves and pillbox hats and suits like the first lady. They weren't very interesting to me. I was pretty sure I knew their stories even though we'd never met.

Some women in the class were very different though and as Mrs. Rhineberg droned on about the different types of filing we'd be learning (alphabetical, numerical, ascending, descending and on and on) I wondered about some of the "different" women.

A tall striking blonde who seemed to be a little bit older than me didn't talk to anyone. She fidgeted with a ring on her left hand. An older woman with long dark hair had a stack of silver bracelets on her arm. They jangled every time she moved. There was an elderly woman who kept coughing and a girl who looked younger than me but who was very clearly pregnant. I was fascinated by these women.

I realized that while everyone in my world was an individual, no one was actually very different from one another. In secretarial school, a microcosm of the larger world, some people were very different. Those differences made all of those women seem exotically beautiful to me. I tried to imagine what their lives were like.

Mrs. Rhineberg talked and talked, seemingly about nothing, then suddenly she said something that caught my interest.

"Beginning on Friday, you'll be starting internships at local offices. Those of you without cars will be set up with businesses you can walk to or on the bus routes. Girls with cars will be given internships you can drive to. You'll be filing and typing and learning by actually working."

There was a ripple of talk among the students. A few of the girls were grumbling but most people seemed interested in the prospect of internships. I know I was.

She said she'd let us know where we'd be going on Friday morning. The rest of the day went by quickly..

As I drove home, I thought about the day. Secretarial school was way more tedious than I'd expected. I'd taken typing in high school, so that would really just be a review. Filing seemed like common sense and I wasn't sure how much I could really learn in that department. I wasn't sure I was ever going to understand shorthand.

Still the prospect of the months ahead with nothing but social obligations to fill them was too much to bear. It wasn't just Rosemary's endless dresses. What happened after that? Surely, my mother would increase her pressure to make me have my own debut. If I got bored enough, I might just cave in and agree to it. Plus I could only go see so many movies. At least at secretarial school there were a few interesting people to see. Also, the internship idea really appealed to me. It surprised me that some students had actually complained about it after class. But I felt, if all I could do was file and type, at least I could do it in a way that hopefully made a difference for someone.

No, I decided I was all in. Totally committed. I wasn't going to tell anyone it was dull. I wasn't going to admit that Mrs. Rhineberg's voice grated on me. I was going to make the absolute best of it.

That night my father asked me first, about the car.

"Did it give you any trouble?" he asked.

"No, it was fine," I said.

I didn't say that it sometimes made a noise like marbles in the washing machine.

"And the class?" he asked, "That went well?"

"Yes, Dad."

"Okay then. Paul said it was a good school."

He walked away as if this were the final word on everything. He didn't really care so much about my experience. Paul had given his seal of approval and that's what mattered.

My mother had more questions for different reasons. She knocked on my bedroom door on her way to go to sleep. I told her to come in and she sat on the end of my bed like she had when I'd been little. I couldn't remember the last time she'd done it. She seemed old to me, sitting there now.

"Did you have a good day?" she asked.

"Sure."

I thought briefly of telling her that there were some interesting women in the class then thought better of it. My mother was all for interesting people when they were just like her. When they were actually interesting, she was uncomfortable. Instead I lied and said "I think I'll learn a lot there."

She seemed to ponder this for a moment.

"It's not too difficult for you is it? I mean it's a long day and I'm sure there's a lot to learn and working can be really hard."

She had no actual experience with this She never had a job. Now my mother is not lazy. In her own way, for her charities and fundraisers and luncheons, she works very hard. But it's on her terms. The thought of *having* to work, of needing a paycheck was frightening to her. She hadn't even been truly comfortable with my babysitting job which had really been no job at all. She didn't feel women should ever have to work. I was pretty sure at least a few of my class mates would disagree with her.

"It's not too hard," I explained. "I'll make sure I get enough sleep every night and I'm certain it will be fine."

"Besides," I couldn't resist adding, "Paul thinks it will be great for me."

I'd said something similar to my father as well. It was a bit of a reach, frankly. Granted, Paul had arranged for me to go and his blessing was all-important to my parents but he hadn't actually said it would be good for me.

"Okay," my mother allowed dubiously, "but if it gets to be too much for you, well, there's no shame in quitting. It's not like you'll ever need a job or anything."

I kissed her on the cheek.

"I'll keep that in mind," I said.

As she left I realized that whether she knew it or not, some small part of her wanted me to fail. That just increased my resolve. Even if I didn't learn a single thing for the next several months, I was totally committed.

Thursday night, before the internship was supposed to start, I had the Peace Corps dream again. This was getting to be a thing. It was a nice dream while I was having it but it made me sad when I woke up and went back to my regular life. Some dreams you forget. Some dreams are awful and it's a relief to wake up. This dream always required a few minutes of re-adjustment when I wished I could go back and live in the dream instead of my life.

In this version, we (whoever "we" were) had finished work for the day. I sat watching the sunset and someone held my hand. We didn't talk much. We didn't really look at one another but having him hold my hand made me feel safe and secure and loved. I knew two things in the way that you knew things in dreams. I knew that I had wanted him to hold my hand for along time. When he finally did, I felt my heart would burst with the joy of it. I also knew that whoever this man was, he wasn't Paul.

⌘⌘⌘⌘⌘

I could scarcely sit still Friday morning in secretarial school. Mrs. Rhineberg was going to send us off to our internships after lunch. She had paired us up so that some of the women with cars could help the one's without. Also, there was a certain amount of accountability in going as a team. Ideally, no one was going to be lazy and do nothing with another student there. In theory, no employer would be able to take advantage of us either.

When the time finally came, I was paired with Anita-somebody-or-other. She said her last name quickly. I asked her to repeat it and still didn't catch it. Finally I just thought, the heck with it. She was the only Anita in the class and she had distinctively ugly cats eye glasses. I figured I wouldn't need her last name.

Anita was one of the socialite girls. I had hoped to be paired with one of the more interesting women in the class but it wasn't meant to be. The elderly woman, whose name I learned was Lucille had been sent upstairs to tackle the cooking school's registration filing. The striking blonde with the traumatized look whose name was Dawn and the Melinda of the silver bracelets each got paired with an anonymous socialite. The pregnant woman had not returned after the first day.

I could easily remember the names of the interesting women but a lot of the other girls sort of blended together for me. They reeked of the sense that they were bored because they were better than this. Their attitudes collectively said, they had better places to be and better company to keep.

They were just killing time. I had been bored too at the beginning of the week. Still, when I figured out what these girls were like, I vowed not to be one of them. I had stopped daydreaming when Mrs. Rhineberg was talking. I took a deep breath every time her inflections or her voice grated on me. I wasn't better than anyone and didn't want to be.

Anita and I were sent to Liberty News. I had never head of the Liberty News. Anita said it was a small weekly newspaper which was nowhere near as good as the big New York papers. I quickly learned that criticism was Anita's special talent. She didn't like Mrs. Rhineberg. (I didn't particularly like her either but declined to say so.) Anita didn't like the idea of internships. Why did we have to leave secretarial school anyway? Why did we have to go God knew where and offer up free labor?

The sun was too bright, the traffic too heavy and she had to stifle a small shriek when she saw my car. I decided I didn't like Anita-whatever-her-name-was.

Liberty News was a short drive from the school and fortunately, they had their own parking lot. A small ceramic sign hung askew over the doorway stating that Liberty News had been established in 1873 and was "New York's oldest continually published mid-sized weekly" whatever that meant.

We climbed a narrow set of creaky stairs and walked into a room, the likes of which I had never imagined. It was noisy. Phones rang and typewrites clacked away. It was grubby, smoky and cluttered. Nobody seemed to sit at their desk for very long. It was a flurry of activity.

Anita-what's-her-name was immediately and vociferously unhappy. I was enthralled. The chaos of it all appealed to some instinct I didn't even know I possessed. After a few unsuccessful attempts to talk to people, trying to find out who was in charge, we finally managed to find a young reporter at his desk. He had his head laid on his arms. He was sound asleep. I hated to wake him up but everybody else seemed to be on the phone, engaged in some loud (and sometimes argumentative) conversations or rushing off like their hair was on fire.

The nameplate on the reporter's desk said Richard Noseworthy.

"Excuse me?" I asked politely

There was no response.

"Mr. Noseworthy?" I asked a little louder.

There was still no response. Anita and I exchanged glances.

"Maybe he's dead," she said in a horrified whisper which implied she'd known this was a bad idea from the start.

At that moment, Richard Noseworthy's phone began to ring. He sleepily groped for it, knocking over a half full cup of coffee in the process. He muttered "It's your turn Delores." While he struggled, still half-awake, to find the receiver, the phone stopped ringing. He mumbled an expletive when saw that the papers on his desk were now covered in cold coffee. Then he abruptly apologized when he realized we were still standing there. He blinked at us stupidly a few times then regained his composure.

"Can I do something for you ladies?" he asked.

"We're from the secretarial school," Anita said, clearly out of patience. "We need to see whoever is in charge."

Richard Noseworthy was more awake now. I smiled at him in a way I hoped seemed apologetic. He had deep circles under his eyes and I felt bad for waking him up and the ensuing calamity that had caused. I also resented Anita's rudeness.

He smiled back at me, ignoring Anita altogether.

"The boss would be Mr. Mike Flanagan." He stood up and surveyed the room.

"That large office, with the big, glass windows, is his," he gestured. "Mike's the guy standing outside it, fighting with the coffee maker. And losing," he added looking downright amused.

I thanked him and followed Anita who'd gone stomping off in Mike Flanagan's direction.

He was indeed losing his battle with the battered percolator. He was swearing and muttering and looked like he was ready to pitch the whole thing across the room. Anita looked horrified and annoyed but she'd continually looked one or the other since we'd left the secretarial school.

I ignored her and walked into Mike Flanagan's line of vision. I smiled and said, "May, I?"

I thought he might say "Who the hell are you?" But he didn't.

"Be my guest. I've had it with this thing. It doesn't even make a decent cup of coffee."

The spindle was slightly bent, so you had to insert it into the basket at an angle, which was why he was having trouble. As I worked, I started to explain to him who we were and why we were there. Mrs. Rhineberg had supposedly set up all of the internships in advance with all of the respective business owners but Mike Flanagan seemed lost.

Finally, understanding dawned on his face.

"Oh yeah," he said snapping his fingers, "Adele Rhine...Rheingold, right? That secretary school."

"Rhineberg, yes," I corrected. "So we're here to..."

Suddenly, Anita screamed. I'd forgotten all about her for a second.

"A mouse!" she shrieked. "I saw a mouse!"

Everyone in the room had turned to look when she initially screamed but as soon as she mentioned the mouse, every body turned back to what they were doing. Apparently mice were no big thing at Liberty News.

"I'm leaving," Anita ranted. "We're expected to work for nothing. This place is filthy and vermin-infested. God knows what else is lurking around here. Take us back to school, Eleanor. Right now."

I looked at her and Mike Flanagan looked at me. A few other people, including Richard Noseworthy had looked back up from their work a second time to see how it would play out.

"No," I said.

"What do you mean no?" Anita demanded. I wondered if anyone had ever told her no before.

"No," I repeated. "We came to do an internship. We came to learn something. I'm not going anywhere right now."

Anita stared at me furiously.

"Fine. Stay here. I don't really care," she spat.

She turned on her heel to go.

"But Anita," I said, with fake innocence. "You don't have a car."

"I don't care," she repeated. "I will call a cab. I will call my father. I will call the police if I need to but I will not stay here!" She stomped back across the office and slammed out the door.

Mike Flanagan gave me a look I couldn't read.

"Not afraid of mice, are you, kid?" he asked.

"No sir, I'm not," I said.

"It's Mike...just Mike," he said. "Save that 'sir' crap for somebody else."

He gave me challenging look.

"You wanted to learn something? You can start, by learning how to make this coffee not taste so goddamned lousy," and he stalked away, leaving me to my own devices with the percolator.

⌘⌘⌘⌘⌘

Mike Flanagan had gone into his office and shut the door. His windows were glass, so I could see him but I had no idea whether or not I should disturb him. He looked sort of busy and annoyed and distracted all at once. I also had no idea what I was supposed to do next. Id assumed we'd have someone tell us specifically what they wanted done.

I had pictured an orientation or an overview or an introduction or something. Still, I wasn't going to leave the news room willingly, until it was time to go. I had gotten a little used to the noise but the sheer amount of different things happening at once still had me enchanted.

I was startled out of my thoughts by a voice.

"He's really a good guy."

"Huh," I jumped a little bit and turned to see Richard Noseworthy.

"Mike. He's really a good guy when you get to know him. And he's one of the best journalists I've ever met."

"Really?" I asked.

"Oh sure. He's just a little distracted these days. His third wife just left him."

"Third?" I asked. "Really? Wow."

I didn't know what else to say. I'd never personally met anyone who'd been divorced even once, no less three times.

"So he's not always like this?" I queried.

"Nah," said Richard. "He's always like this but sometimes not quite so much."

Richard laughed and so did I.

"Richard Noseworthy," he said, extending his hand. "I don't think we've officially met yet. How long was I asleep, by the way?"

"I don't know," I admitted. "Even after everything that's happened here this afternoon, I still only got here fifteen minutes ago."

"Mike hates it when I fall asleep at my desk," Richard grinned, "but my wife and I have 2-month old twins. I don't think I've slept since last spring. Your friend was a little tightly wound," he added.

"She isn't my friend," I said. "Just a fellow student. I actually only met her a few days ago." I rushed on, trying to put some distance between me and tightly-wound Anita.

Richard chuckled and shook his head.

"Well, even if she was your friend before, she sure isn't now."

"That's probably for the best," I said dryly and Richard chuckled again.

"Look, Mike's clearly in some kind of a mood but I have to go in there anyway and ask him about a deadline. If you'd like, I can ask him, what exactly it is, he wants you to be doing during your internship. How's that?"

"That would be great," I said with relief. I small part of me had feared that after Anita's outburst, Liberty News would decide they didn't need a secretarial intern after all.

"Great," Richard repeated and I knew I'd made a friend.

⌘⌘⌘⌘⌘

I didn't say too much to Rosemary or my parents about that first week of school. Rosemary called on Friday evening to see how it had gone. She barely let me get an "okay" out before she launched into a passionate description of some fabric her mother was ordering for her from Paris. Then she dove into an equally passionate apology because I had missed not one but two shopping trips with her that week.

"Paul told me how important this is to you though," she said. "So, promise me you won't feel too bad about missing the shopping. You have to follow your dreams."

I wasn't sure secretarial school was precisely my dream. I also felt a little bit guilty about missing the shopping trips. I'd gone to secretarial school to avoid that very thing but Rosemary was so earnest in her fear that I was missing out.

My mother continued to ask if everything was going well, clearly hoping that it wasn't and that I would come to my senses and drop out. Not a chance.

My father didn't seem to want to know about it at all. He inquired only about the potential safety hazards he was certain lurked in my car. There were probably several of them but he didn't need to know that.

I was looking forward to talking to Paul about my week. He had a sense of humor and he was generally a good judge of people. I was sure he'd be amused by Anita's tantrum and poor Richard spilling his coffee. I wasn't sure what he'd make of Mike Flanagan but then I wasn't sure what *I* made of Mike Flanagan.

Good to his word, Richard had returned from Mike's office that first day with a stack of filing for the subscription department. When I was done with that I cleaned up the coffee station, sharpened some pencils and re-typed some of Richard's coffee-stained copy.

I had watched Mike Flanagan in his glass walled office. He chain smoked. He frequently yelled into the telephone receiver. He paced. At one point in the afternoon, he pulled a flask from the top drawer of his desk and poured an amber liquid into his coffee cup. Despite Richard's assurances that Mike was a good guy, he still seemed a little scary to me. I always valued Paul's opinion and I was eager to hear what he thought.

I had talked to Paul once, on the phone, at the beginning of the week but I hadn't seen him all week. He was putting in long hours at our fathers' law firm getting ready for his first big trial. The basement of their office had been turned into a sort of law library with tons of dusty old books on legal precedent.

Paul joked about the windowless room being like a dungeon. He hadn't been home before 9pm in weeks. He was meticulous in his research and determined to prove that he was a good lawyer. He didn't need to though. He'd long been the golden boy in his family and also in mine. No one thought he could do any wrong yet he worked hard every single day to prove that they were right in those assumptions.

When our Saturday dinner date came, I wore a dress I knew Paul liked and kissed him on the cheek when he opened the car door for me.

"What's that for?" he asked? Despite being a couple forever,

Paul and I never touched much. It didn't seem strange to me. Classmates in high school had complained about their boyfriends being too "handsy" but Paul didn't seem to show much inclination in that department. He was always a perfect gentleman.

"Just trying be appreciative," I smiled at him. "I'm grateful to you for making secretarial school happen."

"Yes, of course," he said distractedly. "I definitely want to hear more about that while we eat dinner." But he didn't sound all that enthusiastic.

He continued to be distracted through dinner although he said he was just tired. Just as I was about to tell him about my week, someone he'd known at school stopped at our table to say hello. Paul politely introduced me, then talked with his former classmate about a professor they'd shared and the prospects for this year's crew team. There wasn't much I could contribute to the conversation as they talked about people I didn't know and things I knew very little about.

As Paul talked, suddenly, I felt like maybe I'd never seen him before. How do you glance at someone who is as familiar to you as your own reflection yet suddenly they seem unfamiliar to you? It's like you were seeing them for the first time ever. I'd been looking at Paul's face since I was a little girl but he seemed different to me tonight. Yet Paul was also the same. Perhaps the different one was me.

I had a memory of my dream with my mysterious hand-holding guy. Not only did Paul seem disinclined to hold my hand, I realized I wasn't all that eager to have him do it. The few times we had held hands, I'd never felt anything near the sense of peace and fulfillment I'd had with the guy in the dream and that was a guy in a dream!

As Paul chatted for a few more minutes with his friend, I realized I didn't want to tell him anything about secretarial school anymore. I wanted to keep my week and the characters in it to myself. I felt possessive of those experiences, suddenly. It made no sense but I felt that somehow sharing them with Paul would diminish them for me. I wondered how I would evade his questions when he asked. But he didn't ask. The former classmate walked away and Paul and I finished most of our meal in silence.

⌘⌘⌘⌘⌘

Not surprisingly, Anita-whatever-her-name-was didn't return to secretarial school. Nobody seemed to miss her. We did discover to our delight, that the cooking school on the sixth floor ran a cafeteria of sorts. It was open to the public and all of the cooking school students had to work there for a few months as a requirement for their graduation. It was like their in-house version of our internship.

On Monday, of the second week of secretarial school. I sat at an empty table intending to call Dawn over. Before I could though, a handful of the socialite girls sat down with me. They were so vapid I could scarcely stand it.

Poor Dawn, ended up sitting by herself. I thought about moving to sit with her but she ate quickly then left. I didn't see her again that day until class was back in session after our lunch break.

The next day, I tried a more direct approach and actually asked her if she was going to lunch before we left our fifth floor classroom.

"Um…yes," she said hesitantly. "Did you need me to get you something?"

"No," I said. "I just wondered if you'd want some company."

"Oh," she said, sounding confused. "Are you sure? I mean, you wouldn't rather sit with the other girls?"

"Not really," I said. "They aren't very interesting," I added. I wasn't trying to be mean to the socialite girls necessarily, I just really wanted to talk to Dawn.

"Well," she giggled nervously, "if you're looking for interesting, I'm not sure that I'm your girl either but I would love the company."

I learned that Dawn was only a couple of years older than me. She was already a widow. Her husband had been in the navy and had died six months before in a helicopter accident. She had two small kids. She and the kids had moved in with her elderly parents after the accident.

"I took a job out of high school as a hat check girl," she said. "That's how I met my husband," she continued wistfully.

She was quiet for a little while then continued.

"I quit when Charlie and I go married. That's the only job I've ever had and it sure isn't going to pay the bills, not that I could probably get it back now anyway," she sighed. "Anyway, I took what was left of Charlie's life insurance money to pay for secretarial school. Thank goodness my parents can watch the kids while I come to school but I sure hope we can get jobs once we graduate."

I pondered how alien this would all seem to my mother. Dawn seemed like a shining, decent person. She was almost heroic to me although she would have said she was just doing what she had to keep her family going. Would I be able to get it together as well as she had if I were in her place? I hoped so but I couldn't be sure. I found that to be a little bit unsettling.

"Thanks for eating lunch with me Eleanor," she said suddenly. "You're only the second person to talk to me since we started school, except for Mrs. Rhineberg," she added. "Some of those other girls are so mean and stuck up. I just don't understand. I tried being friendly but they didn't seem to care."

All at once her face fell. It was such a sudden transformation, I was alarmed.

"What's wrong?" I asked.

"Oh, Eleanor, I'm so sorry. When I saw you sitting there yesterday, I thought you were like them."

Then just as suddenly as she'd become dismayed, her face lit up again.

"I'm so glad you're not one of them," she said, patting my hand.

"Me too," I said.

I hoped she was right about me. I understood where those girls had come from because I had come from the same place. For the first time, that feeling of being an alien who didn't belong to the world she lived in, was a comfort.

⌘⌘⌘⌘⌘

I began to fall into a routine with secretarial school. Although, truth be told, the only parts I was really enjoying, were lunches with Dawn and Friday afternoons at Liberty News. Despite my commitment to try to learn all I could, I wasn't learning all that much at school.

True to Richard's predictions, Mike Flanagan had settled down a little bit. Now, he only seemed to be going in twenty directions at once instead of forty. We didn't have long conversations generally but he did make it a point to leave work for me every Friday.

Richard was terrific about helping me when I didn't know what to do or where to go. On one memorable occasion, Mike left instructions for me to go to the morgue. When I asked Richard about it horrified, he nicely explained that the newspaper's morgue was actually just where old issues and file photos were kept.

It was kind of like my father's basement law library where Paul was spending so much of his time these days. I even met Richard's wife Delores one day. She was sweet. I wondered if Paul and I would ever share the sort of love that Richard seemed to have with his wife.

Mike Flanagan remained a bit of an enigma. Soon to be three times divorced, he was a chain smoker and he drank. I had seen him use the flask on that first day and several times since.

I wasn't a prohibitionist by any means. My parents weren't teetotalers. They had cocktails when they were out with friends. They drank wine with dinner. But the way Mike drank, covertly and at work, seemed to speak of something more desperate. Although, I decided, if *I* knew he was drinking, surely other people knew. Maybe covert wasn't the right word to describe it.

Yet, he never appeared drunk.Plus he was clearly brilliant. Richard's proclamation that Mike was one of the best journalists ever seemed totally appropriate. The man loved words. Sometimes he used bigger words that I had to look up in Yvonne's old dictionary. Sometimes he used words I'd known all my life but he put them together in ways I could never have imagined. His speech didn't always reflect this. His writing always did.

When I was thirteen or fourteen, my class at school had gone on a field trip to the Museum of Modern Art. There had been a whole display of sculptures where artists had taken everyday objects and turned them into other everyday objects.

A tea kettle and a ladle somehow became a chicken. A car's discarded engine block combined with old snow skis to became a forklift. My teacher had dismissed the whole exhibit as vulgar and not very clever but I'd been fascinated. This creating something from something else was amazing to me. Mike's writing was like this. You knew the words he used but you couldn't imagine they could have been combined to create what he had.

⌘⌘⌘⌘⌘

Usually, when I got to Liberty News on Friday afternoons, Mike was on the phone in his office or off somewhere. He managed to check in with me most of the time or at least managed to check in with Richard who would then come to me with a "Mike says you should…" or a "Mike wants you to…"

One day, when I'd been in secretarial school for about a month, Mike was waiting for me when I got to the paper. It was mid-July and the temperature had been in the upper 90's for a week. The air conditioning at Liberty News had never functioned all that efficiently as far as I could tell. It made more scary noises than my Nash and that was saying something.

On this particular day, it wasn't working at all. Work men in navy blue jumpsuits, with Al's Heating/Cooling emblazoned on the back, had pieces of the AC unit apart and spread out on an oilcloth in the middle of the news room.

Mike steered around them and made a beeline for me as I walked through the door. I had a moment of panic. Had I done something wrong? Had they decided that having an intern from the secretarial school was just too much bother? I was enjoying my lunches with Dawn but secretarial school was going to be pretty unbearable without these Friday afternoons.

"Thank God, you're here, kid."

He never failed to call me "kid". I suppose I could have been offended by this but I just couldn't seem to muster up any kind of indignation about it.

"Is everything okay?" I asked, in a voice that was a little more wobbly than I'd expected.

"Helpful Harriet eloped this morning. She's moving to Kentucky or some crazy place to breed horses. Not too goddamned helpful if you ask me."

I tried to wrap my brain around this. Who was Harriet? How was she helping and what did Kentucky and horse breeding have to do with anything?

But Mike had already taken my arm and was leading me to a now empty desk. Slowly, I started to put the pieces together.

"Yvonne eloped?" I asked, still somewhat confused.

"Yeah, Yvonne eloped." Mike said her name like he was only just remembering it.

Yvonne had written the paper's advice column, which was

called Helpful Harriet. I had only ever talked to her once or rather she had talked to me. I had been filing near her desk. She'd had a loud and argumentative conversation with someone on the phone. I had obviously only heard her side of the conversation but what I had heard sounded like

"I don't care what she wants. It isn't her wedding. Well that's not my problem! No, I think swans are completely unnecessary!" Her voice had risen as the argument had escalated.

The argument had ended with her slamming down the phone receiver so hard it had bounced off its cradle, off her desk and into her metal trash basket with a crash.

I had poked my head around the filing cabinet where I was working and said,

"I don't mean to eavesdrop but are you okay?"

She smiled and it transformed her face.

"Don't ever try to plan a wedding when your future mother-in-law is a crazy person. Just elope. It's easier."

Now, apparently, Yvonne had taken her own advice. With dawning horror, I realized what Mike was proposing.

"You want me to write Yvonne's advice column?" I asked incredulously.

"You want me to be Helpful Harriet? There must be somebody else who can do this. A journalist, maybe?" I asked desperately.

"Look, kid," Mike said, "I've got a dockworkers strike, a potential scandal brewing in the mayor's office and the Yankees are playing today. All of my journalists are flat out. You have a brain, kid. You can do this."

"But I've never written," I protested.

"Look," Mike repeated, "it's just advice. Most of the folks who write these letters aren't that bright. If they were, they'd solve their own goddamned problems. They're going to be grateful for anything you can throw their way."

I was sitting at Yvonne's old desk by now and Mike had rolled a fresh sheet of paper into her typewriter.. He pulled a stack of letters out of the top drawer of her desk.

"Look," he said a third time, "just do a few. You're here for your internship time or whatever anyway. If you turn out to be a lousy writer, I won't publish them."

"Okay," I said dubiously.

"Okay," he said with much more confidence.

He stalked away. Twenty seconds later, he was back.

"You can spell, can't you kid?"

Correct spelling, I'd learned in my month at the paper, was a huge thing for Mike Flanagan. He loved words so much he felt you had to treat them with respect. Somehow, in Mike's mind, spelling them wrong was disrespectful. I wasn't sure to whom.

"I can spell," I said.

He still looked a little doubtful.

"If I'm not sure, I promise to look it up," I reassured him, patting Yvonne's old dictionary.

"Okay," he said for a second time.

That time he didn't come back.

⌘⌘⌘⌘⌘

I wasn't sure if I agreed with Mike that the Helpful Harriet letter writers weren't too bright. They seemed like regular people with regular problems. Maybe they just didn't have anybody in their life they could talk to.

I thought of how busy Rosemary was with planning her debut. I thought of how my parents lived in a different world than I did. I thought of how distracted Paul had been recently. I realized I didn't necessarily have anyone in my life I could seek advice from either. It made me sad for the anonymous letter-writers and for myself too. It made me want to help these people I didn't know.

By late afternoon, I'd typed responses for a handful of them. I suggested that the woman with intrusive in-laws should talk to her husband and ask him for some support. I wrote that the boy who loved the girl who didn't know he existed should just ask her out already.

There was a man who'd grown disillusioned with medical school . All his classmates seemed to be pursuing lucrative practices but none of them seemed truly dedicated to helping people. Was the entire profession doomed to succumb to greed, he wondered? Didn't anyone actually care about helping people any more? I encouraged him to stick with it and happily reminded him he could join the Peace Corps and use his talents there.

I was finishing this last letter when Richard stopped by.

"You're smiling," he observed. "That has to be a good thing."

"Hi Richard," I said.

"Mike was on the warpath this morning when he found out about Yvonne. I knew he was going to try to railroad you into this. I wanted to warn you but I've been out on a story for most of the day."

"It's okay," I said. "It's not as difficult as I thought it would be…unless of course these are really awful." I gestured to the pile of typed pages on Yvonne's old desk.

Richard scanned the top sheet.

"No, this is good," he said. "I figured you'd be fine. Mike has good instincts about people's talents. He can usually spot a good writer long before they write a word."

So even though Mike had said he wouldn't publish my responses if they were lousy, clearly he never expected them to be lousy in the first place.

"Thanks," I said feeling a little amazed. I never would have pegged myself for a good writer.

"Listen," Richard said "I'm on deadline with this dockworker strike thing but I wanted to warn you about one other thing."

"Warn me about what?" I asked. I had gone from feeling accomplished and flattered to anxious in about three seconds.

"This isn't just an afternoon of work. In addition to Helpful Harriet, Yvonne covered some of the society stuff and did a lot of the happy little human interest stories too. Mike's going to ask you if you want the job."

Richard left to finish his article and I sat at Yvonne's desk stunned. A job? How was I going to have a job? Could Richard have misread Mike's intentions? I thought not. Mike was all over the place but Richard almost always had a handle on what Mike wanted. I hoped I would have some time to think about it but Mike appeared before I could.

"So," Mike said, sitting on the edge of Yvonne's desk.

"Richard says you've done well here."

Richard had just left. How had they even had time for a conversation?

"They're okay, I guess," I said picking up my slim sheaf of letters.

Mike barely glanced at them.

"Sure, they're fine. And you'll get better, the more you write.

So about that, I want to offer you this job. Yvonne's really gone…don't worry," he interrupted himself. "I was pretty mad at her when she called this morning. I yelled at her. Then I sent her some flowers and a congratulations and everybody's friends again."

I'd been too caught up on my own worries to even wonder how Mike had responded to Yvonne's elopement. I was suddenly touched. It was sweet that he'd made amends with her and even sweeter that he was concerned I'd be worried if he had. The man went from brusque to caring back to brusque faster than I could keep up with.

"Anyway," he continued like he'd never stopped, "this job pays $25 a week. In addition to Helpful Harriet, you'll do some other basic reporting. Not hard stuff, mind you. Fluffy society stuff, weddings, charity benefits, dog shows…you like dogs right?"

"Um…sure. Dogs are fine. But Mr. Flanagan…"

He gave me a stern look.

"Mike," I amended, "why me? Why not run an ad and hire a real reporter?"

"Because, you're here, kid. If I run an ad, then I've got to interview people, which I'll tell you, is horrible. Then I've got to pick a person, call them back, see if they take the job, see if they work out. All that time, nobody's writing Helpful Harriet. Nobody's writing about the dog show and I don't have anybody to write about the mayor's wife's new goddamned hat."

I wasn't sure whether to laugh at that or not. Did they really write news stories about what the mayor's wife wore on her head or was he just trying to make his point?

"The hours are nine to five, $25 bucks a week and if you're not writing you can still do filing and stuff. Come on, help me out here, kid."

"If I was working full-time, I'd have to drop out of secretarial school," I mused out loud.

"Really, kid?" Mike asked. "How much are you learning there anyway?"

I couldn't tell if he was just trying to get me to his way of thinking or he was eerily perceptive. I suspected the latter.

"You already know how to type and file. You're going to learn way more valuable things working here," he insisted.

"Okay," I said feeling like I was falling off a cliff . "I'll take the job."

"Great," Mike said pumping my nervous hand up and down in what had to be the world's firmest hand shake.

"Great," he repeated. "You won't regret it, kid"

I wasn't so sure about that

Driving home that night I was actually thankful for heavy city traffic. It gave me time to think. I felt bad that Paul had paid for secretarial school when I was going to stop going after a month. I suspected that being someplace I wasn't really supposed to be might require some fancy verbal evasion on my part. In other words, I might have to lie. I wasn't very good at it and I'd never had much opportunity to need to. Was I really just giving up like my mother had hoped I would?

A voice in my head that sounded suspiciously like my mother's kept asking, "Really, Eleanor? What do you think you're doing?" As the ride home wore on though, that voice was increasingly overridden by a new voice. The new voice was independent and rebellious. The new voice said, "Why not have a job? Why not do something valuable with your time?"

It eventually occurred to me, that I might not even have to lie too much. Secretarial school had the same hours as Liberty News. My car made it's usual grinding, wheezing noises but it was running and I felt a wave of gratitude to myself for having bought it. Besides, everybody really thought I was just killing time with secretarial school, anyway. They thought I was just like Anita and the other bored socialite girls. They asked me how it was going to be nice but nobody in my life really cared about my experiences there at all. Instead of making me feel neglected, it felt incredibly liberating suddenly

By the time I got home, the critical voice had all but faded away. The independent, excited voice became louder and more familiar. It was my own voice really. The one that had encouraged me to climb trees and make gatehouses into clubhouses and to learn all I could about veterinary medicine. I had just squelched that voice down for so long, I didn't recognize it. But it was my own.

⌘⌘⌘⌘⌘

Mrs. Rhineberg had stopped taking attendance after our first day. She had cashed all of our tuition checks and had settled into happily teaching whichever students where there. She hadn't even made any comment when Anita or the young pregnant woman whose name I never learned, hadn't returned.

However, I was worried that Dawn might feel I'd abandoned her. I'd come to enjoy our lunches and she was the only friend I'd managed to make at secretarial school. But I failed to take into account that she had a totally different mindset about working than I did. I definitely wanted to work but I didn't *have* to work. For Dawn, turning down a job in order to do something else (say, continue lunch with a new friend) wasn't a luxury she could afford.

"Of course you had to take the job," she enthused when I called her. "I'd certainly take one, if someone offered one to me!"

We agreed to keep in touch. I doubt anyone else at secretarial school even noticed I was gone.

I found loved having a job. Writing had not been especially painful to me in school but it had never been my passion either. To my surprise, once I began to work at Liberty News, I found I really enjoyed it. I loved being in the controlled chaos that was the news room every day.

I still felt a little bad about Paul spending money on secretarial school when I didn't finish. I vowed to put a little bit of each paycheck aside and eventually pay him back. Although the newsroom was grubby and noisy, I never did see another mouse. Come to think of it, I'd never seen Anita's mouse either. Maybe she'd made it up. No doubt it was for the best.

I'd never wanted for anything I'd needed when I'd been younger. My parents weren't big on extravagance but I had what I needed. Aside from the brief stint at babysitting though, I'd never had any of my own money either. There wasn't anything particular that I wanted to buy but I loved knowing that it was there and I'd worked for it.

As I'd suspected, no one in my life was suspicious in any way initially. For my part, I felt transformed. It was hard to believe that didn't show on my face. Perhaps it was more of an internal metamorphosis or perhaps the people I loved were just clueless. I didn't know.

Having a job that I loved, had actually enabled me to manage to spend some time with Rosemary on her shopping trips, on the weekends, without wanting to tear my hair out in clumps. She was happy and busily planning.

I debated telling her about the job. She had never been anything but happy for me. Every choice I'd ever made had met with her approval. She had never even chastised me for the thing with the vet. But telling Rosemary meant telling Paul and my parents if only indirectly. That had too many potential complications. I didn't quite feel secure enough yet to share it on that scale.

⌘⌘⌘⌘⌘

On the way home from Liberty News, two weeks after Yvonne had eloped, the inevitable finally happened. My car made a noise like knitting needles in a lawnmower and stopped dead. I was almost home but not quite close enough to walk the rest of the way.

Fortunately, I was out of the city and traffic on this part of the road was light. I tried to start the engine again and nothing happened. I gave it a minute and tried again. This time the engine caught but from the noises it was making, I could guess it probably wasn't going to stay running long.

I managed to half-drive, half-coast another 500 feet or so and pull into the corner of a big parking lot. The parking lot only had a few cars but more were beginning to drive in. Directly across from me was a long low building. In the opposite corner was a large sign on a hefty concrete pillar. "Bowl-O-Drome" flashed in neon. First the "Bowl" lit up in green. Then the "O" flashed on in blue. Finally, the "Drome" winked on in red. Then sign's border lit up with small white stars. The whole business flashed on and off three times then went dark. Five seconds went by and the whole process started again.

I sat there, watching the sign go through several revolutions of flashing. I shook my head and tried to focus. I couldn't just sit in this parking lot all evening being mesmerized by a flashing sign. I had to figure out what to do. I grabbed my purse, checked to make sure I had a dime or two and started to walk toward the bowling alley. It seemed likely that they would have a pay phone.

The interior of the bowling alley was dimmer than I'd anticipated. I stopped, waiting for my eyes to adjust. I stood there blinking confusedly for a few moments.

"Help you?" asked a tall, bald man, behind the counter.

"I'm sorry," I said. I wondered if I was sorry about bothering him, sorry about my car being dead in his parking lot or sorry for seeming like I didn't quite know what was going on. Granted, I'd never owned a car before, so having a car break down, was a novel situation for me but it was more than that.

I'd never been to this bowling alley before. I'd never been to any bowling alley before. My parents were not opposed to sports and leisure activities. My father and Paul had both been on crew teams in college. I'd taken tennis lessons in junior high(not that they'd done much good.) Sometimes I went sailing with Paul's family. These were all acceptable recreation activities. My parents wouldn't have been caught dead in a bowling alley, though. The Bowl-O-Drome was so foreign to me, it might have been one of my Peace Corps countries.

"I'm sorry," I repeated dumbly. "My car broke down. Do you have a pay phone I could use?"

"Sure but it's busted." He pointed toward a dimly lit wall, opposite the counter. The phone's receiver was nicely hung up but the cord that connected it to the box was severed.

"They're supposed to come fix it next week." He shrugged as if he believed this was unlikely.

"Oh," was all I could manage.

"You're welcome to use the regular phone if it's not a toll call. It's not a toll call is it?"

"No," I said, "It would be local."

"Be my guest, then," he said and gestured to the other end of the counter. He turned to re-arrange the bowling shoes on the shelf behind him.

Now, I had to think about who I was going to call. I knew my parents were at dinner with friends. I didn't want to call them anyway, though. My father's primary concern, that entire summer, had been his perceived (and rightfully so, apparently) lack of safety with the car. If he got involved, he might put his foot down about him hiring a driver for me and I didn't want that to happen. There would be no way I could hide the fact that I'd dropped out of secretarial school to take a job.

I knew Paul was still working late as he had been for weeks now. I glanced at my watch. It was 6:45pm. It was way too early for him to be home from the office. I called Rosemary. She would keep a secret if asked, although I hated to ask. It didn't matter though, because nobody answered the phone at her house.

I had a handful of other friends leftover from high school. I didn't really see any of them individually but sometimes we did things in big groups, like go to the movies. Despite being casual friends, they were nice people and any one of them might have come and rescued me.

Unfortunately, I couldn't remember a single phone number. Now that I was being paid to write, I was actually getting pretty good with words. Unfortunately, numbers, including phone numbers seemed to just fall right out of my head. They always had.

I stood, indecisively, with the receiver in my hand so long, the operator came on the line and asked if she could help. I said no and hung up the phone.

The counterman was looking at me, not without sympathy. He seemed like he was debating a question with himself. When I looked up and met his eyes, he appeared to make a decision.

"Not trying to eavesdrop," he said, "but it doesn't seem like you were able to connect with anyone."

"No," I said sadly, "I wasn't."

"I've got a guy coming in for the Friday night league soon. League starts at 7pm. He's a nice guy and a genius about anything with a motor. Wait around until he bowls and he'd probably be willing to help you out."

"Okay," I said nervously. This was turning into a disaster. I didn't want to be a burden on some man I'd never even met. Still, I couldn't think of any other alternatives. I didn't have anyone I could call. It was too far to walk and I couldn't very well stay in the bowling alley all night.

My parents usually stayed out pretty late on Friday nights, so there was still a chance I could get home on my own without creating a problem. I supposed if mister genius with motors couldn't (or wouldn't) help me, I'd have to give in and call my parents anyway but at least I'd bought some time.

"Sit. Be comfortable," the counterman said, gesturing to a group of bar stools around the corner from the counter. So I sat. A few minutes later, the counterman put a bottle of Coca Cola on the bar in front of me. I was grateful for it.

"How much do I owe you?" I asked, digging in my purse.

"On the house," he said and went back to his shelf of bowling shoes.

I sat on the bar stool, watching as people ambled into the bowling alley. They came in groups of twos and threes or individually but they all seemed to know one another. It seemed like an amiable crowd. I was thankful for the soda, not only because I'd been thirsty but it also gave me something to fidget with. I felt seriously out of place.

A man with dark, wavy hair came in with an older woman who looked like him. The woman walked over to alley number ten. The man, who looked to be about my age, stopped and talked to the counterman. The counterman gestured in my direction and both men turned to look at me.

I raised my hand to give a small wave, then quickly put it down, feeling like a dolt. It was too late though, because the younger man was already striding over to me.

"Giuseppe Leonardo Montovani at your service," he said extending his hand.

I just goggled at him. I tried to get my tongue untangled enough to repeat his name back to him.

"Giuseppe..." I managed.

"Leonardo Montovani," he added, then broke out into an amazing grin.

I had has always liked to study faces. I felt like everybody's face had an emotion it went back to. It wasn't that those face couldn't express other emotions. It was just that there always seemed to a place where they were most comfortable. Rosemary's face settled into joy. Paul's face settled in a neutral position, which betrayed little or nothing of what he was actually feeling. My mother's face usually went back to a place of mild annoyance.

I had studied my own face in the mirror for years but I couldn't quite figure out which expression was my home face. Every time I tried to think about it, I got too involved and ended up changing my expression.

I could tell that Giuseppe Leonardo Montovani was used to smiling. He clearly did it a lot. His features just seemed comfortable there. Like that was his default setting.

"Gus," he said still smiling. "Everybody just calls me Gus. Are you the girl with car trouble?"

"Yes," I stammered. You'd think I'd never had a conversation with anyone before.

"And you are...?" he prompted.

I stood there like an idiot. What was wrong with me?

"I can call you broken down car girl but your name is probably easier. Try again? I'm Gus." He extended his hand again.

"I'm Eleanor," I said shaking his hand. His hand were calloused and warm. They were the warmest hands I'd ever felt.

"Ah," he said, as if that explained everything. "Do they call you Ellie?"

My heart was pounding and I couldn't imagine why. I'd never been especially shy and now that I had a job as a reporter, of sorts, I was talking to new people all the time. Talking to Giuseppe Leonardo Montovani seemed to have disconnected my powers of communication.

"Yes," I lied. "Ellie, that's me."

No one had ever called me Ellie in my entire life. I had never thought to call myself that. But suddenly, desperately, I wanted to be called Ellie more than anything.

"Well, Ellie, I have to do my bowling but then I'd be happy to look at your car. See if we can get you going again. Sound okay?"

I don't know what emotion was showing up on my face but I must have looked dubious because he said,

"I'm a mechanic. That's what I do for a living. You looked a little worried there. I mean, I'm not a chef or anything. A chef probably wouldn't be very good at fixing your car, right? Your eggs maybe but not your car, although come to think of it, I fix pretty good eggs too."

The smile never left his face. It made me smile too. There was no way I couldn't. He was totally goofy and it didn't seem to bother him a bit.

"Well, enjoy your bowling," I said finally regaining the power of multi-syllable speech.

"I will, Ellie. I will."

⌘⌘⌘⌘⌘

I watched everyone bowl for a while. Gus bowled on lane ten with the older woman and two other people. Every other lane was full of groups of people bowling but I kept looking back to lane ten. Gus and his family? It seemed likely that at least he and the older woman were related. The whole group was boisterous. They laughed a lot. They touched each other a lot. Playful shoves. Arms draped around shoulders. Light touches on arms. I was fascinated.

My parents seldom touched each other. It had been years since either of them had touched me. I could remember sitting on my father's lap, reading stories when I was very small. I could remember hugs from my mom before I went to sleep but both of those had stopped long before I'd become a teenager.

Rosemary did touch a lot but she was Rosemary. That's how she was wired. Her brother hadn't seemed to get any of her physical affection. Thinking of Paul, reminded me of my dream of the mysterious hand-holding guy again. It made me feel sad and hopeful and anxious all at once.

The alleys remained busy for almost two hours, then people began to leave as they'd come. Gus said goodbye to his companions on lane ten The older woman glanced in my direction, briefly, then walked out the door.

Gus walked over and asked the counterman for a flashlight. He dug one up and handed it to Gus. It was silver and raised circles ran down the length of the handle.

Gus, in turn, handed the flashlight to me. I was surprised by how heavy it was.

"Alright, show me where your car is."

It wasn't hard to find, off by itself in the corner. Most of the other cars were leaving or had left. We walked to Gus' car first. He had a Chevy in robin's egg blue with tail fins. He grabbed a tool box out of the trunk and we went over to my Nash.

He popped the hood. I tried to shine the flashlight where I thought he'd need it. Apparently, I didn't do a great job because after a few minutes, he gently reached up and adjusted the beam's aim. I was struck again by how warm his hands were. Now that it was mostly dark, it had grown a little chilly. I shivered a little and the beam jumped around. I brought it back to where he had aimed it. The flashlight was so heavy that my arm began to hurt a little bit. I tried to keep it steady.

"You're a quiet one," he said.

"Not always," I said, "but you're trying to fix my car, which I appreciate and I'm trying not to ramble on aimlessly, which I fear you might not appreciate. At least not while you're trying to fix my car." I added.

He looked up from the engine and favored me with another chuckle.

"I've got this guy Bobby at the garage where I work. He just never shuts up. Talks from the time he punches the time clock in the morning until he grabs his lunch pail and goes home. Then he probably goes home and talks his wife's ear off. If I can work through his chatter, I think I could probably work through your aimless rambling. Besides, you're an awful lot prettier than Bobby."

I could feel heat rise to my face. Was he flirting with me? I wasn't sure anyone ever had done that before. I managed an embarrassed smile. There was no way I was supposed to be flirting with a stranger in an empty bowling alley parking lot. But I wasn't supposed to have this car or a job either.

Gus had his head under the hood again so I couldn't see his face.

"Is the light okay?" I asked.

"Yup. It's fine now. I'm almost done."

"Really?" I asked.

"Yup. It was a loose …"

He told me what was loose but I knew nothing about engines whatsoever. It went out of my head as quickly as he said it. Just like all those phone numbers. Loose whatchamacallit.

"Look, a couple of other things are wrong here. Do you have a regular mechanic?"

"No. I've actually only been a vehicle owner for a few weeks now," I admitted.

"Well, I could fix it for you. No problem. Could I ask you a favor though?"

"Okay," I said nervously. I was suddenly, acutely aware that we really were alone in the parking lot. I'd always heard stories of women who had been too trusting of strangers. Women who were taken advantage of or worse. But I was totally unprepared for what he actually said.

"Well, my bowling team in there is short a bowler. Normally it's me and my mom and my cousin Dale and my cousin Grace. Actually, Grace was taking my sister Elizabeth's place. Liz is going to have a baby in a couple of months. Anyway, Grace broke her wrist last week. That was Brenda who was here tonight but she could only fill in this week. She's our neighbor. If we don't have a fourth, we'll be disqualified and my mother loves bowling. She'll be really upset if we can't bowl."

I loved how he just talked and talked until he got everything out there. He didn't stammer. He didn't trip over his words. They just sort of flowed out of him. He barely took a breath in between. Amused as I was though, I wasn't really sure what he was asking. At least I didn't think I was going to be killed or accosted in the parking lot anymore.

"So, if I fix your car for you, do you think you could bowl on my bowling team?" he asked.

"Every week?" I asked.

"Yeah, Friday nights," he said. "Until the middle of January anyway. Then we take a break and start all over again in the middle of February."

"I don't know how to bowl," I protested.

"It's easy. I can teach you."

"What?"

This had been a strange evening in the midst of a really strange summer. I felt like I was forever about half a step behind. I couldn't quite keep up. Rosemary and I had seen one of those Godzilla movies once where the big reptile goes trampling all over Tokyo. The movie had been made with Japanese actors but they had added English dialogue later. People on the screen moved their mouths and no sound came out. Then you heard voices but the actors didn't move their mouths. It didn't quite synch up.

I felt that way talking to Gus now. His mouth was moving. I was hearing words but my brain definitely wasn't processing them. Was he really trying to get me to join a bowling team?

"Look, I work all day on Saturdays but you could meet me here on Sunday. I'll fix your car and teach you how to bowl. At least give it a try," he coaxed.

"If you really, really hate it, you don't have to do it. But at least let me show you how."

I had earned a couple of paychecks from Liberty News but realistically, it probably wasn't enough money for car repairs. Despite the fact that Gus had been able to fix my problem tonight without much effort, I knew what kinds of noises my car regularly made. Other repairs probably weren't going to be quite so painless. Plus I didn't know any mechanics (other than Gus). Without the car, there would be no more Liberty News. I had already burned the bridge on secretarial school. No car meant being stuck at home indefinitely and admitting to Paul and my parents that I hadn't been strictly honest with them.

Gus gave me a smile that was like the sun bursting through the clouds.

"Okay, I'll try it. So you'll fix my car. And if I really, really hate it, I'm not going to do it," I said boldly.

"You'll love it," he assured me with grin.

⌘⌘⌘⌘⌘

Sunday came. I could only imagine a conversation where I would tell my parents any part of the truth.

"Sorry, Daddy. Your fears about the Nash are all true. In fact, it's probably even worse than that because I broke down the other night. But it's okay, Mother. I secured repairs. All I needed to do was join a bowling team."

The thought of actually having that conversation really amused me but there was nothing for it; I would have to lie to them.

"Where are you off to, dear?" my mother asked cheerily, on Sunday morning.

The whole thing with the bowling and the car repair and Gus was crazy, I knew. But by Saturday afternoon, I also knew that I wanted to do it all, quite badly. I'm not an especially good liar and I don't always think well on my feet. Still, by the time my mother asked me, I had rehearsed what I would say.

"I'm meeting a friend from secretarial school, in the city for lunch and some shopping. I'm not sure when I'll be back." The last part was true at least.

"That's nice," she said absently. "What's her name? Do we know her family?"

My mother was always interested in people's family connections. She was sure you could judge what a person would be like just based on their family. God help me if that were true. I should have anticipated that she would ask that question.

"Anita Smith," I said smoothly, surprising myself. "She moved here from California not too long ago, so I don't think you know her family."

"Well, have fun, dear." she said absently.

"Any problems with the car?" asked my father, glancing up from a newspaper which was definitely not Liberty News.

"No, sir. Not at all."

It was like I'd been telling lies my entire life. I hadn't. It had never even occurred to me to try to lie about the tree climbing or the vet incidents. Yet there it was. It shouldn't have been so easy to lie to my parents. I wasn't sure if they trusted me implicitly or they just didn't care all that much about what I did. Both prospects were depressing in their own ways. I didn't dwell on them, though. I was out the door and on my way to the car before I could feel too much guilt.

I still didn't know exactly what Gus had done to my car on Friday night but it started right up and didn't sound too awful. I hoped I wouldn't break down again. With luck, he'd be able to remedy the other issues without too much trouble.

I was on time but the bowling alley parking lot was empty when I arrived. Maybe he'd just been goofing with me. He seemed to joke a lot. Maybe this one was on me. I could feel dismay well up inside me. I decided I would give him the benefit of the doubt and wait a few minutes. He arrived just as I was debating whether or not to finally go.

"Ellie!" he exclaimed like we were long lost friends. For a second, I had no idea who he was talking to. I stopped just short of looking over my shoulder.

"Sorry, I'm late. I ended up going back home to get some extra tools I might need," he said gesturing to my car.

"What made you buy this one?" he asked.

"It was the one I could afford," I said with a small laugh.

He responded with a laugh of his own. I don't think I'd ever met anyone who laughed as much as he did.

"Well, that's one of the best reasons for buying a car. Not that it's a bad car, if you love it," he said, seeming like he didn't want to offend me.

I thought about this for a moment.

"I love what it represents. I love that it takes me places, I'd otherwise have to rely on someone else for. I love that I bought it without anybody else's ideas in mind."

"Then you love it," he said. "Let's see if we can get it running a little better for you."

He opened his toolbox and the hood and got to work.

"I can work and talk at the same time," he reminded me after a little while.

"I remember," I said. "You said you had an especially chatty co-worker." I remembered the other thing he had said too, about my being pretty but I didn't say so.

Instead, I asked, "Do you like being a mechanic?"

"Sure, it pays my bills. And it's easy for me. Engines and I have an understanding. I speak their language. I'd like to maybe travel sometime, though," he added as an afterthought.

"Couldn't you travel and be a mechanic too?" I asked.

"Sure," he said.

I thought he might say more but he didn't. A few moments of silence ensued.

"So what do you do?" his voice asked from under the hood.

"Do?" I asked.

"Yeah, do. Do you go to college? Do you have a job? Do you sit on the couch all day and watch TV? Are you a trapeze artist? A witch doctor?" He was off on one of his rambling tangents again.

"I have a job," I said tentatively.

"Was that a question?" he asked. "You said it like maybe you weren't sure."

"I have a job," I said with more assurance the second time.

"So what's your job?" he asked.

"I'm a reporter," I said proudly.

"And you're writing an in-depth expose on bowling alleys and mechanics who hang around in their parking lots, right?"

"You're making fun of me," I said, hoping he wasn't.

"Nah, I was actually making fun of myself a little bit," he admitted. "I think being a reporter is pretty cool. Do you like being a reporter?" he asked more seriously.

"I haven't done it for very long," I admitted, "but yes, I like it."

"You're a recent car owner and a recent reporter. What did you do before all that?"

"Not very much," I said and he laughed.

It took him almost two hours to get my car where he wanted it. Sometimes, we talked back and forth. Sometimes the conversation stalled and we lapsed into silence. Finally, he slammed the hood down and wiped his hands on a rag that hung out of his back pocket.

"You have a few things, that should be fixed eventually but you shouldn't be breaking down again, anytime soon."

"Thanks," I said. "I appreciate it."

"No problem," he said, "but I didn't do it for free, remember? Are you ready to learn to bowl?"

"I guess so," I said, doubtfully.

"Great!" he said ignoring my trepidation. He grabbed my hand in his warm grubby one and led me toward the Bowl-O-Drome.

⌘⌘⌘⌘⌘

I realized no one was at the bowling alley but us. Not only was the parking lot empty but as we walked by the huge Bowl-O-Drome sign, I realized it was dark. Before I could wonder about it, Gus produced a key.

"The pin return machine breaks down a lot," he said by way of explanation. "I fix it and anything else Eugene wants me to fix.," he added. .

I wasn't sure who Eugene was.

"You met Eugene the other night," Gus said. "Tall, bald guy? Passing out the bowling shoes? He's the owner. He's also a distant cousin of my mother's."

Gus flicked on several sets of lights. The Bowl-O-Drome had been dimly lit on Friday night while the bowlers had been bowling. Now light shone everywhere.

"Speaking of shoes," he said and went behind the counter to retrieve us each a pair. I briefly thought about what my mother's reaction would be to wearing shoes that had been on someone else's feet. Despite an aerosol can of disinfectant, I didn't think it would have worked for her at all.

We sat down at the nearest alley. The plastic chairs were all hooked together. Only the ones on either end had arms so they almost seemed more like a bench. I took a deep breath. This had seemed like a really great idea when I was lying my way out of the house that morning. Now, I wasn't so sure.

"You seem really nervous," Gus said to me.

"I told you I've never bowled before," I said, sounding a bit more defensive than I wanted to.

"Don't be afraid of things you don't know how to do," he advised. "Don't ever worry about looking foolish. We all have to learn new things all the time," he continued. "I mean, you didn't always know how to drive a car or be a reporter did you? Were you always good at those things?

Driving was okay but I still wasn't entirely sure, I *was* good at being a reporter despite, Mike Flanagan's reassurances. I didn't say so though.

"I suppose not," I allowed.

"Of course not," he admonished. "How weird would it have been if you were born knowing how to drive?"

I smiled. I liked his sense of humor although I found I couldn't always keep up. He said some things that were just bizarre.

"All right, let's first get you a sense of how the ball feels."

There were several bowling balls in the ball return lane. He picked up and rejected three or four balls before he finally chose one to hand to me. I knew it would be heavy but I was still surprised once I was holding it. I couldn't get my fingers into the holes. He handed me another ball but the holes were way too big. Finally I found one that felt right. I was beginning to feel a little like Goldilocks. He showed me where to put the rest of my hand. I had such a good hold on it, I wasn't sure I'd be able to let it go when I had to.

"You want to take four or five steps up to the line," he said "It matters where you put your feet. When you get up to the line, let the ball go down the alley."

The first time I went too slow and ended up stopping dead at the line. The second time I fumbled the ball and dropped it with a crash. The third time I managed to let it go and it lazily rolled down the gutter.

I looked at Gus helplessly.

"Maybe I'm a lost cause," I said wearily.

"You're not a lost cause, you're a reporter, remember?"

It was another joke but it actually buoyed my spirits. He had no way of knowing how I had come to work at the paper or how I had started out to do something totally different. A few months ago, the car, the job and this afternoon would have all seemed like lost causes. Yet here I was.

We practiced into the afternoon. I didn't think I was going to win any championships in the near future but I had managed to not drop the ball on my foot so that was something.

Later, as we put our bowling shoes back and shut down the lights I asked,

"Am I going to annoy the rest of your team if I'm not any good? It's a competition, right? Points are scored. I assume people like to win?"

"People do like to win," he admitted, "but not us so much. We bowl for fun. My mom started the team with my three sisters. It was a way for them to have some fun after my dad passed away."

"I'm sorry," I said.

"Don't worry," he skipped over my sympathy entirely. "If you really, really hate it, you can quit."

I didn't think I'd be able to quit even if I did really, really hate it.

⌘⌘⌘⌘⌘

I slept poorly again that night. Sleeping poorly was beginning to become an issue. I knew I had to get up to go to work the next morning, so I was aggravated. The more I tried to sleep the less I could. My brain was just too busy. I barely recognized my life now. It's like there were two Eleanors. One did everything everyone wanted her to do except, of course, have a debut. The other one lied and made inappropriate friends and held a job that no socialite girl would want, no matter how bored. I liked the

Eleanor I was becoming. She felt independent and a little bit reckless. The Eleanor I'd always been was a little bit scared of her. I wondered how I would reconcile the two.

I dreamed the Peace Corps dream again. Again, in the dream, Paul advised me not to go. But I went anyway. I made bricks out of mud and taught English. For some reason, Gus was there doing something with an engine.

I dragged into Liberty News the next day.

"God," Mike said, when he saw me, "you look worse than Richard and he hasn't slept in months."

"Good morning to you too *Mr*. Flanagan." I knew the Mr. annoyed him but I'd also learned that he appreciated good banter. As long as I wasn't too disrespectful, my ability to hold my own conversationally was more important to him than egregious shows of respect. He was clearly in charge at Liberty News but he treated the rest of us like equals.

"Well, you better get yourself some of that horrible coffee you make here, because you're getting your first real story today." Somehow, after helping him on my first day, making coffee at the paper became my thing. It wasn't because I was a girl. It was just that I could make the ancient percolator work without a lot of excessive cursing. I didn't even drink all that much coffee.

Richard and Mike had both told me that Yvonne had done more than the advice column but I hadn't done anything other than answer Helpful Harriet letters for weeks. I had told Gus I was a reporter and technically that was true although I hadn't done any actual reporting. I wondered if Gus would have thought that writing an advice column was any less cool than being a reporter.

Mike handed me a slip of paper with a name and address on it.

"You're going to go to that address and talk to this seamstress. She's been making wedding dresses for brides for 45 years. She's about to make her 200th dress."

I thought of Rosemary. Her debut was coming up in just a few weeks now. Her planning had reached a feverish pace. I saw less of her these days but she still called to ask my opinion on things and apologize for shopping without me. It seemed I couldn't get away from endless dresses after all. I must have made a face, because Mike said "It's a nice story, kid. You'll get your first byline."

"Byline?"

"Yeah, byline. As in, 'story by' Eleanor Wilson," he said.

I had a moment of panic. I knew my parents didn't read Liberty News. Frankly, I doubted much of anyone in my town had even heard of it. But what if somebody I knew did read it? I was thrilled to get credit for something I wrote (Helpful Harriet obviously had a certain degree of anonymity to it) but I didn't want my first byline to be my last.

"Got a middle initial, kid?"

"L," I said.

"Fine," he said. "By E.L.Wilson, then. Will that suit?"

I marveled again at his perceptiveness. He didn't ask me the reason for my discomfort. He just picked up on it and helped me fix it. The man was downright scary sometimes.

"That suits me fine," I said.

"Great," he said, "you have a byline but you still need a goddamned story. Go see this nice lady. I need your story by the end of the day."

Maria Alvarez had a tiny storefront shop several blocks away. It wasn't an unreasonable distance to walk but it was, in the shoes I'd worn that day. I decided to take my car. It still made noises it likely shouldn't have but they were a lot less horrible sounding than they'd been. I hoped there would be easy parking. There turned out to be a spot half a block from her shop.

Small bells jingled over the door as I opened it. The shop was not much bigger than my bedroom at home. It was filled to bursting with bolts of cloth and dressmaker's dummies. Lace of every type sat in spools, next to many pairs of scissors. A small enamel bowl held buttons and it's matching larger companion held spools of thread. There was not a single blank surface in the entire place.

I thought about how I had never been exposed to any chaotic environments in my whole life until just a couple of months ago. Liberty News, the Bowl-O-Drome and now this dressmakers shop. Something about the chaos and the clutter drew me to these spaces. Calm and order seemed highly over rated at that point. I didn't want to be in the middle of a war or anything. But my soul craved small amounts of anarchy and I'd never even realized it.

A curtain at the back of the room rustled and a tiny woman with pins in her arm emerged. I did a double-take. On second glance, I could see that the pins were in a pin cushion which was strapped to her arm. Her white hair was in a messy bun. Strands of hair escaped from everywhere. She used the arm without the pin cushion to push some of them out of her face. It didn't do much good.

"When is the wedding?" she asked me.

"What? No, I'm not getting married," I said. "Are you Mrs. Alvarez?"

"Yes," she said. Despite my assurances that I wasn't a bride to be, she seemed to be taking my measurements, visually, anyway. It was slightly disconcerting.

"Mrs. Alvarez, my name is Eleanor Wilson. I'm a reporter from Liberty News. My boss told me you've just finished your 200th bridal gown. We hoped we could do a little story on you for the paper?"

"Liberty News, eh? Mike Flanagan is your boss?"

"Yes ma'am." I had no idea where this was headed.

She smiled a wicked smile.

"I made gowns for Mrs. Flanagans numbers one and two," she said.

"Really?" I asked.

"Sure. They were neighborhood kids all, including Mike. I can't speak for the most recent Mrs. Flanagan," she cautioned. "She wasn't from the neighborhood."

"Mike's a good boy but he drinks too much," she continued matter of factly. "But you know what his real problem is don't you?"

I didn't, but suddenly, I really wanted to. It was always strange to have an outside perspective on someone you knew. Our own perspectives are almost always too narrow. I always like to hear someone else's.

"What?" I asked.

"He's really married to that job of his. He's never going to love any woman the way he loves that newspaper. Sure, he gets lonely sometimes, starts thinking that marriage will be just the thing. Talks some poor girl into marrying him before they figure it out. It never lasts."

"Because they leave him?" I asked. I was moderately scandalized by talking about my boss this way but I couldn't stop myself.

"No. He leaves them. Eventually, he comes back around to realizing that he has only one true love. Then, he tries to let them go gently as he can. Everything is good for a few years until the loneliness catches back up with him. Number three just left a few months ago. I give him another year and a half. Two, tops."

I was fascinated but I could hardly write about Mike Flanagan in my article. I tried to steer the conversation back to her.

"When did you make your first dress?" I asked her.

"1916. I was eighteen and it was the dress for own my wedding."

Richard had handed me a spiral bound reporter's notebook before I'd left the office. "Write everything down," he had advised. "Even if you think you'll remember, write it down anyway."

I pulled the notebook out of my purse and began to write. Once the seamstress started to talk, she just kept going. This was a relief for me. I realized I hadn't really had any decent questions to ask after my first one. Clearly I still had some work to do before I was going to be a very good reporter.

"After I made my dress, my sister wanted me to make her one. Then my cousin. My other cousin. Girls from the neighborhood. I have always been able to sew. I used to make doll clothes for my sister and me when we were small. Soon, girls I didn't even know were asking for dresses. The war came and we had to make do with things we had. I made a dress from a table cloth. I made dresses from flour sacks and still more girls came to me asking for dresses."

She talked about some of her favorite dresses and favorite brides. She had met brides with no money who had bartered things like lamps or jewelry or in one memorable case, chickens, to pay for their dresses. She told me about brides who were difficult or spoiled and some who were really truly in love. She remembered what each dress had been made of and some detail about each wedding. She didn't describe all two hundred of the dresses but I bet she could have. Her memory was amazing.

"The last dress I made was very special," she said.

She had been talking non-stop, but here she paused.

"Why was it so special?" I asked. "Because it was number two hundred?"

"Because it was for my granddaughter," she said. "She was a beautiful bride. About your age."

I smiled at her, encouraging her to go on about her granddaughter and her wedding. Instead she asked, "How old are you?"

" I'm eighteen ma'am," I said.

"Do you have a special boy?" she asked. "Will you be getting married anytime soon?"

I understood that this wasn't a question intended to solicit future dressmaking business. The was a legitimate interest in my life, even though I was a virtual stranger.

"Uh…" I stammered then stopped.

"There's someone who I think wants to marry me but he hasn't asked me officially or anything." It sounded awkward and dopey, saying it like that. As soon as the words were out of my mouth, I wished I could take them back.

If she'd asked me a couple of months earlier my answer would have been more sure. But Paul and I hadn't talked much lately. We kept our weekly dinner date but we didn't do too much more than eat dinner. I was also still haunted by the man in my dream; the one who wasn't Paul. Usually, I tried to reassure myself that it was just a dream and didn't mean anything. It kept coming back into my head though. Finally, I had a whole secret life now. That hadn't been my goal but there it was. I couldn't be sure that Paul wouldn't be hurt when he found out about it.

"I've seen a lot of brides," she said kindly. "A lot of weddings. May I give you a piece of advice?" she asked.

"Yes," I said softly. I was actually afraid of what she might say. I had no reason to be. She'd done nothing but treat me with kindness but I was worried nonetheless.

"Don't *think* that he wants to marry you. *Know* it. Make sure he knows it. And make sure you know that you want to marry him. If you're not sure, if he hasn't asked you 'officially', maybe…" she trailed off here.

"Not being sure can lead to a lot of heartbreak," she finished. "Just be sure."

I returned to the office and typed out my story. I was grateful for Richard's advice about taking notes. When I thanked him for it, I told him that my memory hadn't been as good as I thought it would be.

"It never is," he said with a smile.

I brought my story to Mike's glass walled office just before I left for the day. He glanced it over.

"It's good, kid. Maybe you can make it a little bit longer next time, okay?"

"I can do that," I said.

"I know you can, kid. That's why I hired you. I knew you'd do just fine."

⌘⌘⌘⌘⌘

I wished I had Mike's confidence in my abilities about my bowling. By the time Friday rolled around, it felt like my lessons with Gus at the beginning of the week had been months ago. Despite his advice about not being afraid to try new things I still worried I'd end up looking like an idiot or worse.

Without having met her, I understood that the bowling team was important to Gus' mother. I knew that everyone else on the team was family in some way. How were they really going to feel about some stranger who barely knew how to bowl?

If I could have called Gus and canceled, I might have, but I didn't have his number. I briefly considered not going. He didn't have my phone number either. He didn't know where I lived. What would happen if I just didn't show up? But he had fixed my car. I was starting to see that battered Nash as something of a life line. He had also taken time to try to teach me a few things about bowling. Surely he wouldn't have asked me if he suspected his family would hate me, would he? I hoped not.

Adding to my anxiety, was the fact that I felt I was going to have to do more than lie to my parents this time. There was only so much time I could spend with "Anita". Lunch was one thing but the types of activities the city hosted at nighttime weren't going to win my parents' approval.

Granted, I wasn't actually headed to the city. It also wasn't like my parents didn't let me go out. I went out with Rosemary or Paul or school friends all the time. It was just that my mother knew all of those friends and their parents as well. She was always curious about who I was with. I just didn't see any way I was going to be able to explain this. I felt like sneaking out was going to be my only option. Unfortunately, not only was I not sure I'd be able to carry it off, it just seemed so trite. Wasn't 'sneaking out' what teenagers did in the movies?

Despite my qualms, it was surprisingly easy. I said I was going to bed early. I said that we were learning an awful lot in secretarial school these days and I was wiped out. I said I would read for a while then just go to bed. I had done that for years in my early teens, anyway, so it didn't seem wildly out of character for me. It had been a long time since they'd checked on me once I was in bed.

I had the growing feeling that my parents just weren't all that interested in my life. Of course they wanted me to do the right things. They didn't want any indiscretions or transgressions on my part. I'd known that for certain after the incident with the vet. But as long as they thought I was doing the right things, they really didn't care about the details.

Aside from the thing about the debut and the lack of college they really didn't impose any of their hopes and dreams on me. Did they even have hopes and dreams for me, other than to see me marry Paul? I didn't know. Later, I wondered if I should have just told them the truth.

It was perfectly simple, to climb out my bedroom window. My room was on the first floor at the back of the house. I was thankful my father had demanded that I not park the Nash in the driveway. You couldn't even see the gatehouse from the front part of the house.

The only difficulty I encountered, aside from the racing of my heart, was that the lane leading up to the gatehouse was somewhat dark. It would have been better earlier in the summer but it was heading towards the fall now and getting darker earlier. I vowed to stash a small flashlight in my purse.

The Bowl-O-Drome parking lot was busy tonight. Not like the last two times I'd been there. I parked and watched the neon Bowl-O-Drome sign go through its lighting stages a few times. What was it about this sign? It was almost hypnotic. I could have watched it for hours. Especially if it meant I didn't actually have to go in and bowl. Finally, I took a deep breath, and walked into the bowling alley.

I wasn't sure if the counterman recognized me or not. He didn't show any signs of remembering me. He just asked me for my shoe size. He handed me a pair of bowling shoes and turned to the next customer. It was pretty busy though and I looked slightly less pathetic than I had the week before when my car broke down.

I looked over to lane ten and Gus was already walking toward me with a goofy smile on his face.

"I thought maybe you weren't coming," he said.

"I thought maybe I wasn't either," I said with a nervous laugh.

"Come on," he said again taking my hand in his. His hand were always warm. It was like he had his own inner furnace or something.

He led me over to lane number ten.

He introduced me to a boy who looked like he was a little younger than me. He wore a black turtleneck sweater. His face was flushed and he looked like he was uncomfortably warm.

"Ellie, this is my cousin Dale."

No matter how many times Gus called me Ellie, I still had to think for a second who he was talking to. I shook Dale's hand.

"Cool, man," Dale said cheerily. "Glad you could fill in. I can't believe my sister broke her stupid wrist and *his* sister," he gestured to Gus, "is the size of a house."

Gus' mother shot Dale a look and Gus punched him in the arm.

"She's going to have a baby, moron," Gus said, not without affection. "It's not like she ate a thousand jelly donuts."

"I love my cousins," Dale said. "You know that. And my wonderful aunt," he added, putting an arm around Gus' mother's shoulder.

"Ellie, this is my mom, Maryann."

"It's nice to meet you," I told her. "And you too Dale," I added, realizing I hadn't acknowledged his introduction earlier.

"Thanks for bowling with us," Maryann said graciously. "And don't worry. We're just having fun. Gus tells me you've never really bowled before."

I didn't know if she knew about the private lesson Gus had given me on Sunday.

"Well, I'll certainly try my best," I said.

"I'm sure you will," she said.

Gus and Dale talked and joked and teased one another. Maryann sometimes laughed at something they said or made a small comment but she was much quieter than her son and nephew. I barely said anything. I was busy trying not to dump the ball into the gutter, trying not to drop it on my feet and hoping to remember to let go before I launched myself down the alley.

A few times, I looked up to find Maryann, not precisely staring at me but studying me. It was like she was trying to decide what I might do next. If she could figure it out, she was probably ahead of me. I could now say, "I'm on a bowling team," and it felt very strange indeed.

At one point, Dale said to me, out of the blue, "Oh Ellie, you and Gus should really come to my reading tonight. It's at the cafe just down the road. You'll have a great time. Please say you'll come."

"Reading?" I asked "What are you going to read?"

"Poetry, man. I am a poet and I am reading some of my work tonight."

For once, the smiled had temporarily left Gus' face. He actually looked a little worried.

"I'm not sure that's really something Ellie would enjoy..." he began dubiously.

Maryann was looking at me again, clearly wondering what I was going to have to say about it.

"I'll go," I said decisively. "It sounds like fun. I'd like to hear your poetry," I told Dale.

Gus looked surprised but pleased. Maryann smiled at me. Dale positively beamed at me. I had apparently given the correct answer.

When we were finished bowling, we went to the parking lot, Maryann wasn't going to go with us to the cafe.

"I've heard this one talk in poems since he was a little thing," she said and ruffled her nephew's hair.

"I was a 'little thing' back when you could do that," he said, pulling her hand away. He seemed to appreciate the affection though, rather than be truly annoyed by it.

"I've been hearing you since we were both 'little things'," Gus grumbled, good-naturedly. "Why do I have to go?"

"Ellie thought it would be fun," Dale reminded him.

Maryann went home. Dale took his own car to the cafe. Gus had ridden with his mother to the Bowl-O-Drome, so he climbed into my Nash.

"It might not be fun," he warned when we were both in the car. "Dale's poetry is really pretty awful."

Just as his smile looked incredibly comfortable on his face, so too did his worry look completely like it was unused to being there.

"How bad could it be?" I asked.

He raised his eyebrows. "Oh you've never heard his poetry. It's pretty bad."

"Don't worry," I told him.

"Okay, boss," he chuckled, the smile returning to his face. "If you're not worried then I'm not worried. Just don't say I didn't warn you."

⌘⌘⌘⌘⌘

The cafe was a strange place. It wasn't precisely a bar. It wasn't precisely a diner. It was a little bit of both and neither. A sign behind the long counter proclaimed, "Best Coffee In Town." and another said "Breakfast All Day". Yet no one was eating tonight. There was a stage with a drum kit and some small amplifiers. Small tables, each with three or four chairs, dotted the floor. Someone had dragged one of the chairs up on the stage. A handwritten sign was taped to the microphone which said "Poetry Tonite".

Gus and I sat at a table toward the back of the room. Dale gave us an enormous smile and a wave from where he sat with what I assumed were some of the other poets. Dale looked much cheerier and far less angst ridden than they did.

I smiled at Gus. His face still held traces of anxiety. I wanted to make him smile. As if I could somehow put his face back where it belonged. Anything but smiling just looked wrong for him. He met my gaze and shook his head.

"I'm not sure why Dale hangs around with these guys," he said gesturing to the other poets. "They write poetry about death and the pointlessness of existence."

"You've come to hear them all before?" I asked.

"A few times," he admitted. "Dale's my cousin and a good kid. This isn't really my thing but I try to be supportive."

"What does Dale write poetry about," I asked.

"Kittens," Gus said shortly.

I had no idea if he was joking or not. I didn't get to find out either because the lights dimmed and the first poet welcomed us and began to read from a small notebook.

The poets were all about 16 or 17. The all wore chunky black sweaters, and black pants. A couple of them sported berets. When they started to read, I realized that one was actually a girl although most of them were guys.

I had never really thought much about poetry one way or another. It was hard for me to judge whether or not is was actually any good. It was definitely dark. Some of the kids wrestled with some pretty serious issues in their poems. I wondered if they really had experienced such grief, loss and loneliness or if they just had especially vivid imaginations.

Each poet read for 5-10 minutes. Dale went on toward the end. He did indeed talk about kittens. And sunrises. And the ocean. One of his poems went:

Sunrise
Inhale the cool morning air
Inhale the universe.
Get lost in the sky
Embrace Forever
Never forget love
Each day the day begins again
Sunrise.

I didn't think it was awful at all.

His imagery was especially vivid but his subject matter varied so widely from his companions, I thought for sure he'd be teased. But when he'd finished reading, he left the stage to applause. A voice from the poet's table yelled, "Express yourself however you can. Don't let the man tell you what's in your soul!" Which caused applause to break out again even harder.

We stayed at the cafe for almost two hours, drinking Cokes and listening to the poets. Finally, the lights came on. They were done. Dale came over to tell Gus that he would be back out in a few minutes, to drive Gus home.

"I liked your poetry, Dale," I said. I really had.

Dale beamed like he'd won the lottery and turned back to his cousin

"I told you, you guys would have fun."

"I suppose we did," Gus admitted.

Dale said, "I'll be back in ten minutes," and walked back over behind the stage, presumably to confer one more time with the other poets.

When I turned to look at Gus he had an expression I couldn't read. The worry had drained from his face but his normal grin hadn't replaced it. Instead, he wore a look of wonder which I didn't understand. Maybe he was surprised that Dale was so well-liked by his peers too?

"What?" I asked.

"You," he said.

"What about me?"

He was making me a little nervous now, although not necessarily in a bad way.

"You have got to be, hands down, the best sport I've ever met."

"I'm a sore loser at Scrabble," I teased. This wasn't true. Sore loser wasn't really part of my personality but I was trying to keep things lighthearted.

"I doubt that," he said. "I don't see you being a sore loser about anything." He continued.

"You didn't have to come tonight to hear Dale and his crazy beat poet friends but you did. Plus, you joined the bowling team…you didn't do too bad for your first time tonight, by the way."

"Thanks," I said, a little embarrassed. "I had to join the bowling team though, remember? After all, you did fix my car," I reminded him.

"I'll let you in on a secret," he said.

"Yes?" I asked, hoping I sounded calm. My heart was pounding for some reason.

"I would have fixed your car anyway, even if you hadn't agreed to join the team. I just wanted an excuse to spend more time with you. The bowling team was the only thing I could think of so you didn't get in your old, clunky Nash and drive right out of my life."

Neither of us said anything for a few seconds.

"You're not going to quit the team, now, are you?" he asked, panicked. "I wasn't really trying to trick you or insult your car..."

I put my hand on his.

"I'm not going to quit," I assured him. "I didn't really, really hate it. It was actually kind of fun."

His smile was back and he gave my hand a squeeze. I pulled it away. Now I was making myself nervous. All of the sudden he looked serious again.

"Go out with me, Ellie. On a real date. Not here. Not at the bowling alley, but a real date. Next week, after bowling."

The next week was Rosemary's debut. Fortunately the main event was scheduled for Saturday but there was also a party scheduled for Friday night and Sunday afternoon. The Saturday and Sunday ones weren't going to be a problem but I figured I was going to have to book it home as soon as bowling was done next week and I was still probably going to be late.

Dropping out of secretarial school, taking the job at Liberty News and joining a bowling team had all been crazy turns my life had made lately but they didn't hurt anyone. True, I hadn't been outstandingly honest in order to accomplish them although much of the dishonesty had been lies of omission. But going a date with

Gus, real or otherwise might actually hurt somebody.

What about Paul, I thought. But what about him? We were not formally engaged. We hadn't even talked about it since just before secretarial school when he'd insisted he wasn't ready to think about marriage yet. Since then, we'd barely talked about anything. That was my fault too, I knew, but for the first time ever, my future with Paul had a degree of uncertainty to it.

Gus' face had fallen. I'd taken too long to answer.

"I'm sorry. It's okay if you don't want to…" he began.

"No, I want to," I rushed. I realized that I really did want to go on a real date with him. "It's just that next weekend is really messy. I have a friend who's making her debut."

He looked at me blankly.

"She's having her debutante's ball," I said. "You know, her whole coming out party and all the other parties that go with it?"

"Debutante's ball," he said slowly, as if he still wasn't really sure what it meant.

"Yes," I confirmed. "Next weekend. But we could have our 'real date' the following weekend, couldn't we?"

"Sure we could," he said, sounding happier.

Then, his face changed again and he looked dismayed. He had the most expressive face ever, even though only his smile seemed like it was really comfortable there.

"Ellie?" he asked. "That's not your scene, is it? Debutante balls and society parties?"

"I can't stand them," I told him and I was never happier to have it be true.

⌘⌘⌘⌘⌘

The week before Rosemary's debut flew by. I promised her I'd be available every single for night that week for whatever she needed. Last minute shopping. Dress consultations. I didn't have any of the party-planning skills Rosemary shared with our mothers but I offered to do whatever I could.

I knew Rosemary had tons of other friends but I still couldn't help but feel I'd abandoned her a little bit. I was trying to make up for it, the week before her debut. I wasn't sure how I was going to cover for my absence Friday night while I did my bowling but I hoped an idea would come to me.

Sometime, during that crazy week, the first batch of Peace Corps volunteers left for Africa. President Kennedy stood in the Rose Garden at the White House and personally thanked them for going. He said that if they had chosen to stay home the would have undoubtedly been successful in their own pursuits but they were doing a great thing by traveling overseas to help other people.

I didn't dream about the Peace Corps every single night but I'd had variations of the dream several times now. Always, somebody told me not to go. Usually, it was Paul although it had been my mother in at least one version of the dream. Always, I went anyway. Always, I woke up feeling just a little bit sad.

Work was also busy. My story on Mrs. Alvarez the seamstress had gotten some positive feedback, mostly from former brides or other old ladies from her neighborhood. Mike decided I could handle some more. In addition to keeping up with the Helpful Harriet letters, I began to write about other things. There was a neighborhood horticultural society meeting, an award winning quilt and as promised, even a dog show.

One day, Mike assigned me a story about a local racehorse who had won dozens of races. He was going to live at some farm upstate. Not Mike. The horse.

"I'm not supposed to interview the horse, am I?" I joked with Mike. Mike Flanagan was still a little scary to me but I knew he appreciated humor.

"Cute, kid. Very clever. No, you're not supposed to interview the horse. Go to the racetrack. See if you can find a jockey, a trainer, anybody who worked with the horse. His name is Royal Bounty, by the way. Just in case you do get to talk to him" he said sarcastically.

When I got to the racetrack it was really quiet. There were no races that afternoon. It normally would have been in a flurry of activity on a race day. I found a couple of jockeys eating their lunch but neither of them had ever ridden Royal Bounty. Nobody else seemed to be around.

I went to the stables. Maybe I was going to have to interview Royal Bounty after all. I had been smart enough to snag a couple of sugar cubes from the coffee station at liberty News. I gave these to Royal Bounty and gave his neck a pat. He looked at me to see if I had any more treats for him. Once he realized I didn't, I wasn't very interesting to him anymore.

I was getting ready to give up when a voice behind me startled me.

"He's a beauty, isn't he?"

I turned to see a gray-haired man with a black bag.

"He is," I agreed.

"I just have to check him out one more time," the man said. "Give him a clean bill of health before he goes into retirement."

Then he gave me a funny look.

"Do I know you?" he asked.

"I don't think so," I said but I introduced myself anyway.

"I *do* know you," he said with a smile "Did you ever become a veterinarian Miss Wilson?"

It was the same vet I'd endlessly badgered that summer. It was the vet I'd helped to deliver the foal. I was happy to see him and even happier to find out he'd cared for Royal Bounty for several years. As he worked on the horse, he told me all sorts of things about the races Royal Bounty had won and the only few he'd ever lost. He was a wealth of information.

"Thank you so much," I told him when he'd finished examining Royal Bounty. The horse had a health certificate and I had my story. "And thank you too for letting me follow you around that summer. My parents weren't thrilled but I had a wonderful time. I hope I wasn't too annoying."

"The pleasure was mine." He smiled at me. "I liked having a young assistant. Any chance of you going to veterinary school?" he asked.

"Probably not," I admitted.

"Shame," he said and walked away.

⌘⌘⌘⌘⌘

At the end of the week, Richard asked me if I had weekend plans. I told him about Rosemary's debut and associated parties. At least he didn't seem horrified like Gus had.

"Talk to Mike," Richard told me. "We don't usually cover your part of the world but Mike says you're producing really good copy now. You could cover it. We sometimes need the society stuff as filler. If there's room, he might run it."

I appreciated his confidence in me but there was no way I going to ask Mike about covering Rosemary's debut. I hoped Richard didn't get it into his head that he'd be doing me a favor and ask Mike himself. Writing as E.L Wilson was probably safe for me in this corner of the city. The only people I really knew here either worked for Liberty News or already knew I did, like Dawn. But writing about something so close to home both emotionally and geographically wasn't going to work. E.L. Wilson was not such a great reach to Eleanor Wilson. Eventually, in the winter, secretarial school would be officially over and I'd have to come clean about my other life. I hoped to keep it a secret until then.

Friday night arrived before I knew it. Rosemary's debut obviously required much more formal attire than I would have worn to the bowling alley. I figured I'd have to stash my dress for the debut in my car and change in the Bowl-O-Dome's bathroom before I left. The timing was just that tight. Rosemary herself ended up giving me a reason to leave for the Bowl-O-Drome in the first place.

One of Rosemary's other friends asked if Rosemary had bought flowers for her mother. The friend said she'd bought flowers for *her* mother to present to her at her debut. It was almost 6pm. Bowling began at 7. Rosemary's Friday night party was technically scheduled for 8pm but I figured if I could manage to show up by 8:30 or so, I'd be okay. Rosemary herself was planning on being fashionably late and wouldn't get there until almost 9 even though the party was at her house and only required going downstairs.

"Oh my!" Rosemary exclaimed "Flowers for my mother are such a wonderful idea. She has been so helpful. But I didn't think of it sooner! How am I going to do it now?"

"Stay here. Keep getting ready," I advised. "I'll try to find a flower shop that's open late." I was pretty sure I'd seen one right next to the cafe where Dale had read his poetry. Now I just had to hope they'd be open.

"I can't make you do that, Eleanor," Rosemary said, now genuinely distraught. "You'll miss helping me get ready and how will you get ready yourself?" she lamented.

"Don't worry about me," I said. "It looks like you have plenty of support here and I'd like to help. Besides, I can get ready pretty quickly."

Both of these things were true. I did want to help her because I hadn't been around much lately I also could get ready much faster than most of the girls I knew. Not being obsessed with dresses and shoes made my choices much easier. I just didn't fret that much over how I looked. Usually whatever I'd managed to come up with seemed good enough to me. I felt a little twinge of guilt though because I knew I had ulterior motives. I wasn't just hoping to be helpful.

For a minute, I wasn't sure she was going to let me go. I held my breath. Then, she launched herself at me and gave me a big hug.

"Oh Eleanor, thank you so much. Flowers will mean the world to my mother."

I'd been right. There was a flower shop right near the cafe. They were just closing as I got there but I convinced the shopkeeper to let me in. I picked a rose bouquet someone had already arranged and set on the counter as a display. The whole transaction took less than five minutes.

Thankfully, the weather was just slightly chilly. The flowers wouldn't suffer any ill effects in my car while I bowled.

I didn't tell Gus or my other new teammates that I was really time crunched. Yet somehow, we finished sooner than we had the previous week. It was just enough time to get me back. As I was about to leave Gus said, "I know you're busy this weekend but do we still have plans for next weekend?"

He wasn't just asking if we still had plans. He was also trying to make sure I was still okay with the real date concept.

"Yes. Of course. It'll be fun." I hoped I sounded sincere but I was feeling flustered. I had to get through Rosemary's debut before I could really even think about it.

"Okay," he said. "We'll bowl like normal on Friday, then we'll do something on Sunday." He sounded casual, nonchalant.

"Okay," I agreed. We stood there awkwardly for a moment. Then, I went off to change in the bathroom. I left the Bowl-O-

Drome feeling like Cinderella hurrying home from the ball before her carriage turned back into a pumpkin. Of course I was hurrying *to* the ball. At least it wasn't mine.

I got back just before Rosemary made her entrance. My mother gave me a perplexed look and I shrugged as if to say I'd explain it to her later. I'd probably have to embellish a little, about having to drive around looking for an open florist's shop. At least the basic story was the truth.

Rosemary was luminous the entire weekend. She was social and gracious and sweet to every single person who was there. She'd been born to do this. She'd been practicing at parties for year. She was the perfect young society lady. Plus, unlike many of them, she was sweet. It seemed she would have her choice of eligible bachelors.

I thought of Anita-what's-her name and her friends. I couldn't imagine any of them behaving as nicely as Rosemary did that weekend.

Paul was in attendance for all three days, of course, but I didn't really get to talk to him until the barbeque on Sunday.

I was standing alone, wondering if my mother would renew her efforts to get me to consent to my own debut after Rosemary's success. I wanted this even less than ever, now. I was happy that Rosemary was happy. She actually went beyond happy and seemed to float on a cloud of bliss. But it wouldn't ever be bliss for me.

I don't know if I ever could have come to terms with being a debutante. I was definitely a goner as soon as Kennedy came on TV that spring and announced his Peace Corps. That had really kicked up all of my restlessness again. I had done well for a long time but this didn't seem like my life anymore. I felt like more of an alien than I ever had. I had a job and a bowling team now. If I could make those work, maybe the Peace Corps wasn't all that farfetched. Even if I never managed to join the Peace Corps, I knew for certain I would never be able to make the debutante thing work for me now.

Paul interrupted these musings.

"I brought you one of those cupcakes you like," he said offering it out. "You know, the ones my mother makes with the raspberry filling?"

He smiled easily. I took the cupcake feeling that somehow it was a peace offering.

'Thanks, for helping Rosemary this week," he continued. "She said you've done a lot."

"Not so much, really," I said cautiously. "You know with secretarial school and all."

"You've still really helped her," he insisted "How is secretarial school going?" he asked.

"It's going well," I lied, hoping he wouldn't ask for specific examples of how.

"I've been really self-absorbed lately," he admitted. "I wanted to apologize for that," he added.

"I've just been trying to prove myself at work. I know I don't need to. I mean, it's your father and my father but it's because I don't need to, that I feel I need to, if that makes sense."

It did, actually.

"Anyway," he continued, without waiting for me to comment, "I want to hear more about you at our next dinner date. And I think I'll have some good news for you very soon."

"Great," I said not really sure that it was. I couldn't imagine what his good news would be. I realized, with a pang, that I still didn't want to tell him more about me.

The next week at dinner, true to his word, he was different. In fact, he was even different than he'd been before he'd started working so many hours. Where he had always been reserved and relaxed, he now thrummed with an excitement.

"So how is secretarial school going,?" he asked again

"It's going well," I said again. He always asked in the same way. I always answered in the same way. "It's going well," was my standard answer whenever anyone asked about secretarial school. Fortunately, no one asked all that often. I wondered what I'd have to make up if anybody ever asked for more information.

"That's excellent," Paul said. "You may even be able to help me in the future."

"How?" I asked.

"Well, the case I've been working on has been a huge success. My father thinks that if I get a few more of these big cases under my belt, then I may have a great political future. Of course, if I run for office, I'll need a wife," he said looking insufferably pleased with himself.

This was new for him. He usually erred on the side of humility. I decided I liked humble Paul better than pleased-with-himself Paul.

"So, you hang in there, a little while longer. It'll mean me putting in some more long hours but I should be able to do some great work. We might be able to get married next summer, then I'll be able to start my political career. Isn't that wonderful?"

Although I'd always assumed I'd marry Paul, his new attitude implied that I wanted nothing else in my life. I could be an accessory wife and maybe do his secretarial work too and that was supposed to leave me feeling incredibly fulfilled. It was supposed to be my dream in life to make his life happy. Didn't anybody care if my life was happy? I hated feeling resentful but once it seeped into me, I couldn't seem to dispel it.

"That's wonderful," I said without enthusiasm. "If you ever need to cancel our dates, so you can work," I gestured vaguely around the country club restaurant, "I'm okay with that."

Paul briefly took my hand and squeezed it. His hands were cold. He released it just as I realized that the mystery man who held my hand in my dreams had exceptionally warm hands.

"You're the best!" Paul exclaimed "I'll let you know if I ever need to cancel."

I didn't feel like an alien then. I felt completely invisible.

⌘⌘⌘⌘⌘

The next day was my "real date" with Gus. I'd been feeling bad about it right up until my talk with Paul. A better person probably would have told Paul that she wasn't sure she wanted to marry him at all, next summer or anytime else. But that hypothetical better person was more sure of herself than I was. She was more self-assured and composed. Maybe she knew exactly what she wanted and more importantly how to get it. I hoped someday, to be that better person. Right now, I was relieved that I didn't have to make any difficult choices just yet.

Gus wanted to pick me up but it wasn't going to work to have him meet my parents obviously. I was also embarrassed to have him see my house. After he'd made nervous comments wondering if I was a debutante, I wanted only to be a regular girl. My house was too big for a regular girl to live in. That girl who lived there would have to have money and I didn't think she'd appeal to Gus at all. He reluctantly agreed to meet me at the Bowl-O-Drome.

On Friday night after bowling, we had agreed that we would meet at ten on Sunday morning. He said he had something he wanted to show me. He said I should wear good shoes for walking. He was at the Bowl-O-Drome before I was. He jumped out of his car and regally opened my door. I'd only just barely turned off the engine.

"Ellie Wilson, welcome to your real date," he said. "We have flowers," and he handed me a bunch with an elaborate and goofy bow. "We have a picnic," he said gesturing to a basket in his back seat. "We have blue skies," he said pointing upwards and we're going to have a lovely day."

He took my arm and we walked the handful of steps around my car and over to his. Then he stopped exaggeratedly and opened the passenger side door. He grinned like an idiot. His good humor was contagious and I couldn't help but smile back. He was smiling today. His face looked comfortable.

We took lots of little back roads. We twisted and turned. I had no idea where we were and I couldn't have gotten back to the Bowl-O-Drome if my life had depended on it. The leaves were changing color but the day was pleasantly warm. It really was beautiful.

"So, Miss Reporter, what are you reporting on these days?" he asked.

I was thrilled that he'd asked. I never got to talk about Liberty News with anyone but Richard and Mike Flanagan. Since they both worked there, it wasn't the same. I was also really happy that I had something in addition to Helpful Harriet to talk about. Not that Helpful Harriet was bad. I actually enjoyed answering those letters. I felt like I was actually helping people but I liked doing some actual reporting too. I told him about my retiring racehorse and the quilt competition and some of the more interesting Helpful Harriet letters I'd answered.

Finally, we drove down a tiny road which wasn't much more than a glorified path. We crossed a small stone bridge. The road ended in a small, unpaved, open space. It couldn't even rightly be called a parking lot but we parked there anyway. No other cars were around. He insisted on coming around to open my door.. He grabbed my hand and we went off down a path that led to the woods. I'd had my momentary qualms about feeling unsafe that first night in the Bowl-O-Drome parking lot but I couldn't imagine feeling unsafe around Gus anymore.

I was glad he'd thought to remind me to wear shoes I could walk in. We hiked up the path. Every so often the trees opened up into a wider clearing, then the path would narrow and wind away again.

Twice, Gus grabbed my arm and steered me around a fallen tree or a hole in the ground. Gus pointed out various types of trees and flowers. He showed me an old beehive and a squirrel nest. He seemed to know a lot about nature for a mechanic. Finally, the path sloped back down and just ended.

At the bottom, built into the hill, was an opening framed in stonework. It was about four feet high. I couldn't see how far back it went. Gus pulled a small flashlight out of his pocket.

"What is it?" I asked.

"Mystery cave," he said excitedly.

"Mystery cave?" I asked perplexed.

"Come on, I'll show you," he said. "You're not claustrophobic are you?" he asked worriedly.

"No, but…" I said uncertainly.

"It's great," he insisted and dragged me through the entrance.

We really had to crouch down in order to walk in. Even with his flashlight turned on, I could only see murky darkness ahead, After a few steps, we were able to stand up straight but we walked for another fifteen or twenty feet before we came to a big open chamber. Sunlight streamed in through a round opening in the chamber's ceiling.. I touched the stone wall reverently.

"It lines up with a constellation," Gus said. "The Pleiades. I've never been here at night though," he said sounding wistful.

"It's not really a cave, is it? Some one built this?" I asked.

"Yes. It's man made but nobody knows who built it or why." He looked at me as if he was trying to gauge my reaction to all this. I had an amazing sense of belonging to the universe. It was incredible to feel like everything was connected and that I was a part of that. You'd have thought it would have made me feel small but it was just the opposite. I walked a couple of steps so I could stand directly under the opening. I walked around the chamber feeling the cool stones under my hands.

"This is amazing," I said. "I've lived in Connecticut my whole life and never heard of this." Not that I was tremendously well-traveled even in Connecticut.

"There are hundreds of these throughout the Northeast," Gus said. "Dozens of them, right here in New England."

"And nobody knows what they're for?' I asked. "Did the Indians build it?" I wondered aloud.

"Maybe," Gus allowed. "That's one of the theories, anyway, but nobody knows for sure."

It was a great mystery. I was fascinated. Nobody in my family appreciated a good mystery. My mother especially, wanted to know what was going to happen and when. If those things could happen in the same ways all the time, even better. The unknown, change and uncertainty were all things to avoid, not to embrace, in her world.

I loved the mystery of this place though. I felt a little giddy, like maybe I was perched on top of a windy cliff instead of inside a small stone chamber.

Gus was still watching me. "Do you like it?" he asked. "I hoped you would think it was interesting."

"I love it. It's amazing," I repeated. Then, I surprised us both by turning and giving him a huge hug. "Thank you for showing it to me."

I couldn't have even imagined such a place existed no less that I would be enchanted by it. Gus, it seemed, knew both, which was somewhat astounding to me We walked back through the chamber's entrance and hiked back toward his car. I looked back longingly a couple of times.

"Let's eat some lunch," he said. "We can always come back for another look, if you want, after we eat."

He had packed sandwiches, apples, potato chips and a vacuum bottle full of coffee. I'd worked up an appetite hiking up to the mystery cave and the sandwiches were surprisingly good. We spread a blanket in the grass to eat.

"If you mind sitting on the ground, we can eat in the car," he said.

"I don't mind the ground," I said. I had sat on the floor a lot when I had my babysitting job. I didn't have much opportunity to sit on the floor these days but I liked it. It made me feel more grounded somehow.

When we'd each finished two sandwiches I asked him, "How come you know so much about everything?"

He thought I was teasing. "Well I don't know about *everything*," he said a tiny bit defensively.

"You know about bowling and fixing cars and archeology and sandwich making," I said. "You know about plants and trees and things in the woods. You just seem to know about all sorts of different things," I said. Then in case he was still feeling defensive, I added, "I admire it really. Sometimes I feel like I don't know about much of anything at all."

"I'm just interested in all sorts of different things, I guess," he admitted, warming up again. "I read books. I like to talk to people about things. I think it's important to keep learning even if you're done with school."

"What do you think of the Peace Corps?" I asked. I'm not sure what I'd originally intended to ask him but that hadn't been it. That had come out of my mouth before I'd even had a chance to think about it. For a minute, he looked perplexed, like he was trying to remember what it was.

"Oh yeah," he finally said. "That's the President's program to send volunteers to emerging nations, right? I think it's a great idea."

I couldn't believe he'd said "emerging nations" just like the president had. It made my heart want to burst.

When we'd finished eating, he leaned back on his elbows.

"Do you ever watch clouds, Ellie?"

"Watch them do what?" I asked. "You mean like for changes in the weather?"

"Well certainly, that's practical," he admitted. "But I meant just watching them. They shift, they change. Sometimes they actually look like things. It's not necessarily practical," he admitted "but it is very relaxing," he said.

I leaned back on my elbows like he did. Fluffy, fair weather clouds moved slowly in the sky. They just looked like clouds to me at first. After a little bit though, I did began to notice shapes. I pointed out one I thought looked like a fish. He showed me a dog, then a pine tree. Eventually, my neck was sore and I just lay down on the blanket, on my back. He did the same. We laid there for a long time just watching the clouds, occasionally pointing out an interesting one to one another.

I hadn't noticed any particular tension in myself before then. I felt the tension of deadlines at the paper and I felt nervousness at the bowling alley hoping I was doing okay by my teammates. But I guess I had gotten so used to these things that they didn't feel abnormal or uncomfortable. Lying on the blanket, looking at clouds with Gus I realized that all of the tension had drained out of me. I noticed its lack of presence. I felt like I could just float away like one of those wispy clouds we'd been watching. Finally Gus stretched and sat up. I sat up too, hugging my knees.

"Is there any coffee left?" he asked.

I unscrewed the lid. A little bit of brown liquid sloshed around in the bottom of the vacuum jar.

"I'm not sure how warm it still is," I said dubiously.

"Doesn't matter," Gus said. "I'll drink coffee hot or cold or any way really."

I poured the rest into the cup and handed it to him. He gave me a great smile and drank it in one gulp.

"Sorry," he apologized after he finished it. "I didn't ask you if you wanted any more."

"I'm fine," I said Except for the mornings, I could take or leave coffee.

"I want to show you something else. Are you ready to go or do you want to go see the mystery cave again?"

I remembered how I had been reluctant to come back down the hill.

"No, it's okay." Then I added, "We could come back sometime, right?" I loved the mystery cave but I was also curious about the other thing he wanted me to see.

"Sure," he said beaming. Then he was serious. Serious never failed to look out of place on his face. It made serious look more serious somehow.

"Are you enjoying our 'real date', Ellie? Because I know some girls who'd be mad because we hadn't gone to a fancy restaurant or out dancing or something. They wouldn't have considered a hike to the mystery cave and cloud watching a 'real date'." He looked at me expectantly.

"I know those girls," I said. "But I'm not like them. At least, I don't want to be. I love the mystery cave. Really."

He looked relieved. "Well, it was kind of a test," he admitted.

"A test?" I asked.

"I thought you were the kind of girl who would appreciate a cave and clouds kind of day. I wanted you to be that kind of girl. If it turned out you weren't really that type of girl after all, well…" he trailed off.

"What?"

"Well, we still could have done the bowling thing but I'm not sure I would have wanted any more 'real dates'." He looked mortified but I was possessed with a sudden boldness. I wasn't going to let it go.

"And now that you've discovered that I am a cave and clouds kind of person? Now what happens?"

"Now? First I do this," he said pulling me into an embrace. "Then this," he whispered as his lips touched mine.

Paul had never given me anything more than a brief kiss on the lips. More often it was a peck on the cheek or nothing at all. I wouldn't have said I would have even known what to do. Girls at school had always made a big deal about kissing but I would have told you I didn't know anything about it.

I needn't have worried. Gus knew what he was doing. It was like being swept into a strong current, I was just carried along. When he pulled away, I was breathless and a little dizzy. When my thought process finally worked again I had the silly thought that it had been Kiss with a capital K He held me at arm's distance and studied my face.

"Was it okay that I did that?" he asked.

"Do it again," I said. "And I'll let you know."

He did.

⌘⌘⌘⌘⌘

The other thing he wanted to show me was just as surprising to me as the mystery cave. We drove for another 45 minutes or so, mostly in silence. There was no distress in it. I think we were both processing what had happened. We had evolved to a different place in a short time with that kiss. Maybe it was inevitable that we would have gotten there sooner or later. I didn't know. I'd never thought much about destiny. We sat close together on the Chevy's front seat. Toward the end of the drive, he took one hand off the wheel and held mine.

We stopped next to a huge meadow. In the middle of the field was one ancient tree. Hanging from the tree was a giant tire. It looked like it had come from a truck. The tree reminded me of the one I'd fallen out of so long ago when I broke my arm.

Birds sang. Wildflowers bloomed here and there. There was no house. No barn. No sign of anybody anywhere.

"Who does this belong to?" I asked in wonder.

"I don't know," Gus admitted. "My oldest sister Barbara brought us here after our dad died. Sometimes we'd spend all afternoon just taking turns on the swing. I don't know how she discovered it. She was always really secretive about it. She would only say that it was a special place and it didn't matter. I haven't been here in a few years. I wasn't even sure it would still be here," he admitted. "But someone tends it," he added. "The rope has been replaced since the last time I was here."

"I'm sorry," I said, "about your father, I mean. How old were you?"

"Barbara was seventeen by then. Carmen was thirteen. Liz was nine and I was six. Liz and I were probably the only ones little enough to appreciate it," he gestured to the swing, "but we all took turns on it, even Barbara."

"I love to swing,' I said "but I haven't in years.. Play isn't exactly a priority in my family," I admitted feeling a little sad.

"I think playing makes us happy. We're supposed to be all grown up and everything but little kids play all the time and they're really happy. Adults don't play much and a lot of them seem pretty unhappy." Then he got a wicked grin on his face and took off running for the swing. I ran after him

We took turns pushing each other on the swing. Everything seemed to make us laugh. We'd settle down, then something would set one of us off and we'd go off into spasms of laughter again. I laughed so hard that my ribs hurt. We laughed over nothing at all. I could have stayed there all day.

Finally, the sky began to cloud up. All those white fluffy clouds that had looked like little animals a few hours ago began to look gray and a little bit menacing.

"We should go soon," he said eying the sky. "Looks like it's going to rain and it's getting chilly."

It was but I hadn't noticed until he mentioned it. I wondered if he would kiss me again. I was afraid he wouldn't. I was afraid he would. I couldn't imagine feeling bold enough to kiss him first..

It started to drizzle on our way home. By the time we got back to the Bowl-O-Drome it was raining harder and almost dark.

"I had a really nice day," I said as we pulled into the parking lot. Nice seemed sort of insufficient to the task but it was all I could manage to get out of my mouth. I felt like I was mildly concussed but not in bad way.

At any rate, he didn't seem to care about my lack of eloquence.

'Me too," he said. "See you here Friday?"

"Unless I decide I really, really hate it," I teased.

"I sure hope you don't," he said seriously. I got the impression we were talking about more than bowling.

⌘⌘⌘⌘⌘

The day after my first real date with Gus, there was someone sitting at my desk at Liberty News.

She was about my age. She had a shock of blonde hair and bright pink lipstick. She was chewing gum in an annoying way.

"Can I help you?" I asked.

"I'm supposed to be answering some of these Helpful Harriet letters," she said, snapping her gum. She didn't seem to be doing anything at all, other than loudly chewing her gum.

"Who are you?" I asked, feeling panic and annoyance both rise in my chest, competing for my attention.

"I'm Candy," she said with her own annoyance, as if it should have been obvious to me.

Just then, Richard walked by my desk.

"Hi Eleanor. Mike wants to see you in his office," he said over his shoulder. "I've got to go to the police station for some info on a story. Coffee later?"

We'd gotten into the habit of chatting by the coffee pot just after lunch. I asked his advice all the time. He always gave it using some example of a story he was working on or had already written.

"If I'm still around later," I muttered wondering why this Candy person was sitting at my desk. Richard hadn't seemed to think it was odd that this person was sitting at my desk.

Mike Flanagan had grown a little less scary to me in the four months since I'd first seen him cursing at the coffee percolator. He was still abrupt sometimes. He still sometimes drank his lunch. He was still brilliant. Sometimes, he joined us at the coffee pot in the afternoons. My talk with Mrs. Alvarez, the seamstress, had made him seem more sympathetic to me. He still intimidated me, just not quite so much.

I still usually tried to wait until he was out of his office to talk to him. When I did have to knock on his big glass door, I often did so timidly. I always hesitated if he was on the phone, which he frequently was. Now though, I was mad. I had worked really hard. He was firing me? I knew that my anger was only a thin veneer over my terror. A few months before I couldn't have even imagined having a job. Now I was absolutely horrified that I might lose it.

Mike was on the phone when I got to his office. I knocked on his door but didn't wait for him to motion me to come in. I stomped in, arms folded. I must have looked scary to him for a change because he told whoever was on the other end of the phone that he'd call them back.

"Eleanor," he began.

Fueled as I was by panic, I lost all semblance of manners and interrupted him. I never interrupted anyone.

"You're firing me?" I asked more shrilly than I'd intended. "There's a person at my desk saying she's going to write Helpful Harriet. *I* write Helpful Harriet," I said as if he didn't already know that. "I've missed three months of secretarial school," I lamented. "I don't think I'll be able to go back."

This earned a rare smile. Where Gus smiled all the time, Mike Flanagan almost never smiled. Mike's default face was aggravated. Mike Flanagan was smiling at me now.

"I certainly hope you don't go back to secretarial school," he said. "I admire your passion," he added. "But don't waste it on me. Save some for your new assignments."

You can blow up a balloon and not tie it off. If you let go of it, it rapidly deflates and flops around a little bit. This is what I felt like: flopping around helplessly then deflating.

"My what?" I asked, confused.

"You're a really good writer," Mike said. "I need you on bigger stories. Helpful Harriet is just holding you back. Plus, you type well, you've helped out with the filing and you make that terrible coffee we all drink. You do a lot around here." He paused at that point, gauging my reaction.

" I'm promoting you, kid. Not firing you," he added, in case I continued to be dumb.

"Oh." Realization was beginning to dawn. "So you interviewed people?" I asked.

"Which, I've told you. is horrible," he reminded me.

"And you hired somebody else to write Helpful Harriet so I could write bigger stories?" I inquired.

"Isn't that what I just said, kid? Would you prefer that I fire you?" He was teasing, I hoped.

"No, no," I rushed. "Thank you Mr. Flanagan…Mike. You won't be sorry." I assured him.

"I haven't been so far, kid. I gave you a new desk across from Richard. He's been a good mentor for you. He'll be able to help you if you need it. Come back in about fifteen minutes and I'll have your first new assignment." He picked up the phone and begin to dial, shooing me away as he did.

⌘⌘⌘⌘⌘

My first real news story was about a local fire station. Liberty News really was all about its neighborhood. The fire station had originally been part of a larger station also in the neighborhood. Someone had decided to split this one off in a different part of the neighborhood for better coverage. The station had some cast off equipment. from the original, bigger, station but needed some new equipment to really be effective. The issue was going to go before voters soon. The fire chief was afraid they wouldn't understand how desperately the new equipment was needed.

It was interesting to be able to talk to the fire chief. People came in so many different types and personalities. People like Anita and the bored socialite girls of her ilk found that variety annoying. They seemed to feel that everyone should behave and think exactly as they did. But I loved people's differences. I always wanted to hear what they thought even if I didn't agree with them exactly. I was going to like being an actual reporter.

I continued to plead exhaustion with my parents and sneak out on Friday nights to bowl. The first Friday after our real date, Gus and I were a little bit strange with one another. We bowled as usual and I was actually getting better. We were a little bit awkward though. For my part, I know, I was thinking about our kiss and how warm his hands were. Dale was oblivious to the slight tension between us. He chattered happily about school and his beatnik friends. Maryann seemed to notice though. She didn't say anything but that woman didn't seem to miss a thing. Gus and I made plans again for Sunday.

By late afternoon on Saturday, I was beginning to feel guilty. I wasn't certain where Gus and I were headed but I could no longer tell myself we were just pals. He was no longer just a guy who had been nice and fixed my car. It probably never been true. I'd found him attractive from the first time I'd seen him walk into the Bowl-O-Drome.

I figured Paul deserved an explanation of some sort. Every day I spent with Gus made marrying Paul seem less likely. It wasn't that I thought I was going to marry Gus *instead* of Paul although that made for a sweet little fantasy. After all, was only just getting to know Gus.

I just didn't know how Paul and I were going to make each other happy. I thought of Richard and Delores again. They had seemed like they fit together somehow. I wasn't sure at all how Paul and I fit together, especially now that he had political aspirations.

Could I tell Paul I was uncertain about our future without telling him the rest? Maybe I could just address my feelings of unease without bringing up Liberty News or the Bowl-O-Drome or Gus. It seemed disloyal to Paul to mention them but it seemed disloyal to myself not to.

I figured I would have to tell him something and the sooner the better. I decided I'd talk to him that very night. I had no idea what I'd actually say. "Hey, this guy at the bowling alley fixed my car and then we went on a date with caves and clouds and I'm just not sure about us anymore", didn't seem like my best choice but I vowed to tell him *something*. I like to think I really would have. But the phone rang, just after 4pm on Saturday afternoon. My father answered it.

"Certainly, I'll tell her," he said. "No, I'm sure she'll understand. Keep up the hard work, son." he said, then he hung up.

"That was Paul," my father told me. "He still has some research to do at the office and he's going to have to cancel your dinner date tonight."

My father looked at me to see if I would complain. I had never been a complainer and I wasn't going to start now. I felt only relief.

"I understand," I said. "In fact, I told Paul he could cancel any time he needed to. I know that he has things to do."

"He works so hard," my mother commented. "He'll make a wonderful husband, Eleanor."

I didn't tell her that I couldn't imagine that he would be *my* wonderful husband. By the time I saw Paul again though, the urge clear my conscience and reveal all, had passed.

⌘⌘⌘⌘⌘

It was Thanksgiving before I knew it. Paul and Rosemary always spent the holiday with family and were usually gone for the entire weekend. My parents and I spent the holiday together.

My parents are both only children. All four of my grandparents passed away when I was small or before I was born. I am an only child. Sometime I think life might have been different with a sibling. Paul and Rosemary had fundamentally the same upbringing that I'd had but they had each other. Thanksgiving always seemed like an impossibly lonely holiday to me. My parents and I sat at a big table in our big dining room. I always thought it was too big for just the three of us.

Did other people's parents ask for more information about their lives? I didn't know. You tend to think that all families are like yours. You might wonder or fantasize that they could be different in some way but it's impossible to know for certain. Maybe other daughters would have been more forthcoming with information too. It wasn't like I was sharing much with them.

"How's secretarial school going?" my father asked. My mother didn't really ask anymore. She had wanted me to just quit. When she realized I wasn't going to, she didn't see any point in asking the question. If only she knew the whole story. Yes, I had indeed dropped out but not because it was difficult and not because I wanted to achieve more ladylike pursuits.

"It's going well," I said. "I'm learning a lot," I added to my standard response.

"Those skills will come in handy when Paul begins his political campaigns. You'll be able to help him," my father observed.

My mouth was full of turkey, thankfully, so I didn't have to respond. I smiled and nodded in a way that I hoped made me seem ultimately agreeable. As if helping Paul with his political campaigns was all a girl could want.

When I finished chewing my food I said,

"Yes, Paul said something about that too."

I was feeling lonely and not especially thankful after dinner, so I took a walk. I knew there were things I could and should be thankful for. I wanted to be but I was feeling grouchy.

I walked down the lane toward my car out of habit more than anything else. I was thankful for my car. Granted, it wasn't much to look at. It also made some horrible noises although it made fewer of them now that Gus had spent some time with it. Still it connected me to Liberty News and the Bowl-O-Drome and Gus. I was thankful for all of those things. Liberty News had saved me from certain boredom. The Bowl-O-Drome had let me grow in a way I never would have expected and Gus...well he was Gus.

I loved spending time with him. He made me laugh. I could always count on him to express a point of view which hadn't occurred to me before. Maybe I was falling in love with him. I wasn't sure whether I should feel grateful for that or not. It was a little bit frightening. It definitely made life more complicated. Still, I figured you should never be sorry about love no matter how difficult it made things.

I continued to walk. I came to the tree I had fallen out of as a little kid. It had seemed so much taller then. I thought it was funny how your perceptions change. I had been standing on a branch about ten feet up. I remember hearing it snap. The next thing I knew, I was on the ground. For a few seconds, I felt no pain. I'd had the wind knocked out of me and I couldn't breathe. I lay on the ground looking up at the tree branches. I could hear the other kids calling for help. They seemed far away and for a moment I actually thought I was dead. Then my breath came back along with an unbearable pain in my arm which was twisted under me in an awkward way.

I leaned up against that tree now. I thought briefly about climbing it again but thought better of it. I had worn a skirt to dinner and tree climbing in a skirt was probably a bad idea. I thought of Gus' tire swing on the tree in the middle of nowhere.

I heard honking all of the sudden and looked up. Several geese, in their signature 'V' formation, were flying overhead. It was like they were calling back and forth to one another. It always made me a little bit sad to see them at this time of year because I knew they were leaving rather than coming. I always got a little thrill if I saw them in the spring because I knew they were returning. I didn't really like winter but I loved the spring.

I walked and walked all around our property until it was dark and my feet hurt.

⌘⌘⌘⌘⌘

Liberty News didn't put out a paper the week of Thanksgiving. Richard said it would be hellish to catch up on Monday but that's just how it was. There was also no bowling on Friday night because of the holiday. The previous year, had been my senior year in high school and I'd hung out with friends from school for much of the weekend. Many of those friends had gone off to college or were doing different things. Without the common tie of school, I'd lost touch with most of them.

I knew from the mimeographed sheet Mrs. Rhineberg had given us on our first day that there was no secretarial school on Friday either. I called Dawn.

"I'm thinking of coming into the city," I told her. "Would you want some company?"

We had talked on the phone several times since I'd gone to work for Liberty News but I hadn't actually seen her since leaving secretarial school in the summer.

"Oh, Eleanor. That would actually be wonderful but we'd have to hang out at my house, if that's okay. The kids are both getting over a cold," she said, then added with dismay "Or maybe you won't want to come. I don't want you to get sick."

"Don't worry," I assured her. "I hardly ever get sick." It was true. I stayed relatively healthy most of the time. Still, she could have told me they had the plague and I still probably would have gone., I was feeling desperate to get out of the house.

Dawn and her family lived on the third floor of an old brownstone apartment. It seemed like it had once been elegant. Time and neglect had worn it down though. Now it was comfortable and clean but shabby. I buzzed the buzzer from the front step and Dawn came down to let me in.

"I'm so glad to see you," she said giving me a big hug. "It's been an awful week. Everyone was sick with this cold; the kids, my parents, me. It was miserable. Plus this is our first

Thanksgiving without Charlie. I thought it would be so hard for the kids but they're doing okay. I'm the one who is a mess."

"I'm sorry," I said. "Can I do anything for you?" I asked, concerned.

"No," she said sounding better. "It's just great that you're here."

She introduced me to her parents who sat at the kitchen table drinking tea. Her children were three and five. They were sprawled out on the living room floor coloring.

"They're not usually this quiet," she said with a laugh, "well, the kids aren't, anyway. My parents are always pretty quiet."

"How is secretarial school going?' I asked her. I wasn't really missing secretarial school but I was curious about what they were learning. Was I missing anything? I asked the question in the same way my father and Paul asked me but I actually wanted to know.

"I really hope it wasn't a waste of Charlie's insurance money," she lamented. "I'm learning a few things but Mrs. Rhineberg seems to go over the same things over and over. And the internships are done."

"Done?" I asked incredulously.

"Yeah. I guess they were only supposed to go for six weeks, although Mrs. Rhineberg made it sound like they'd continue for the whole class, so I was surprised when I found out they were ending. I liked mine," she added wistfully.

"I was working at an accounting firm. The girl I was paired with didn't do any work at all. Every Friday, we got there and I did all of her work and mine too. She just filed her nails. I didn't mind, though," she added quickly. "I don't mind working. Maybe they will think I was a hard worker and hire me once we graduate."

I hoped they would hire her. I was annoyed by this nameless socialite twit who'd made my friend work so hard while she'd done nothing. I was really glad though, that I'd accepted Mike Flanagan's job offer. I don't know that I would have survived secretarial school without the internship. I was beginning to wonder about Miss Cavendish, whoever she was, in Paul's office. Nobody seemed to learn much in secretarial school yet she had raved about it. Either she had known absolutely nothing to begin with or she'd been more bored than I could imagine.

Dawn and I chatted all afternoon. Her parents were nice people. Her kids reminded me some of the kids I'd babysat for. Dawn was surprised when I got down on the floor and colored and built block towers with them.

"You don't have to do that, Eleanor," she said sounding worried.

"I want to," I assured her. "I love kids." I remembered Gus' comment about adults not playing enough. Sometimes I guess you had to borrow a kid if you wanted to play more.

Being with Dawn's family felt really comfortable. My own family seemed like a bad fit for me. I'd always felt that way, just never so keenly as I did now. How was that even possible? How could a person be born into a family, spend their entire life there (so far) yet still not feel like they belonged there? How could you be that out of alignment with your own family?

Finally, when Dawn announced it was time for the kids to go to bed, I realized I had to go home. I would have been perfectly happy to never leave.

"Secretarial school is done in mid-February," Dawn reminded me as I was leaving. "Keep your ears open. Please let me know if you hear of any job openings at the paper or wherever."

I told her I would. Inside, I had a moment of panic. Mid-February was less than three months away. When Paul and I had talked about secretarial school being 'several months', that had seemed like a huge chunk of time. Now it was more than half over.

I was sure that the better Eleanor I aspired to be would have found a way to fix everything. She could have kept her job, her bowling team and Gus all while not angering her parents or hurting Paul's feelings. She could have gotten Dawn a good job to boot and insured that Rosemary would marry the perfect man. Well, Rosemary, at least. always landed on her feet. She wouldn't need perfect Eleanor's help.

I wasn't that better version of myself though. Not yet. Maybe not ever. The Eleanor I was just took a deep breath and hoped three months would be enough time for everything to work itself out.

⌘⌘⌘⌘⌘

The Sunday after Thanksgiving Gus and I had a serious talk. We had agreed to meet as usual and we'd gone to a movie that afternoon. The movie wasn't very interesting. We sat through it but Gus was definitely not himself. Instead of seeming relaxed like he usually did, he was both awkwardly stiff an fidgety at the same time. After the movie was done, and we were in the car on the way back to the Bowl-O-Drome, I asked him what was wrong.

"You like me right?" he asked.

"What?" I asked in disbelief. "Of course I like you. I like you a lot."

"I know it was a holiday and there was no bowling and you had family things going on," he began. "I get the logistics of all that. But I *missed* you this weekend. I really just wanted to hear your voice."

"I missed you, too," I said, unsure where this was going.

"Did you?" he asked pointedly. "Because I still don't have your phone number. I can't call you. I still don't know where you live because you've never let me come to your house. I have to meet you at the Bowl-O-Drome. It's like you have to be sneaky. It's like you have a secret life or something."

Ouch. He was right on the mark yet he wasn't. How could I explain that he and the Bowl-O-Drome and Liberty News were my secret life? That my other boring life with Paul and my parents and their fancy house was supposed to be my real life. I wasn't hiding them from Gus so much as hiding Gus from them. Yet that was terribly unfair, wasn't it? I had thought I was protecting everyone but maybe I was just alienating everyone, especially him. I, of all people should have known better.

"I'm really sorry," I said. "I'm not very good at this. I never really went out with anyone like this before." It was lame and didn't really explain my behavior but it was also true. We pulled into the Bowl-O-Drome parking lot. He stopped his car next to my Nash. He turned off the engine and shifted on the car seat so he could really look at me

"You've never had a boyfriend?" he asked surprised.

"Not like this," I said. That was true, too. I reached over and kissed him, hoping I could say what I was incapable of articulating in words.

That week, I called the phone company. I used money from my Liberty News paycheck and had my own phone line installed in my bedroom. I made sure my mother would be at her bridge club and my father would be at his office. I called the paper and explained to Mike that I had to wait for the phone technician.

"Do what you have to do, kid," he said. "Just don't forget to come back tomorrow."

If nothing else, at least Gus would be able to call me.

⌘⌘⌘⌘⌘

I had barely talked to Rosemary since her debut. It had gone so well, she was fighting off all sorts of eligible young men. That's what my mother said anyway.

"It's good you have Paul," my mother had said, implying that my insistence on not having a debut would render me hopelessly unattractive to any decent man. Thank goodness, Paul had taken pity on me. She didn't say this last part but that's what I heard nonetheless.

Rosemary called me the Monday after Thanksgiving. In typical Rosemary fashion she was apologetic for ignoring me.

"I'm so sorry for neglecting you, dear Eleanor," she began.

"It's okay, really," I insisted.

"No, it's not," she countered. "But we're going to remedy that on Saturday. I think I've met the love of my life. Warren is charming and sweet and so considerate and really, really cute." She was gushing.. Before I could ask more about the wonderful Warren, she went on.

"I want us to double-date this Saturday. Warren and I. You and Paul. Paul's met him already, of course, but I want you to approve although I'm sure you'll just love him," she plunged on.

I was a terrible friend. We barely even had anything in common anymore yet she still wanted my approval. Was I just not very loyal? Rosemary was so devoted I was sure she'd be heart-broken if I didn't like Warren. Yet when was the last time I'd shared any detail of my life with her? Never mind all that had happened since the summer; I'd never even told her about my dreams of the Peace Corps. She was probably the only person in that circle who would have been supportive yet I had hoarded my secrets away like treasures.

"Paul's been working really long hours," I said. "In fact, he's had to cancel our dates for the last few weeks."

"I talked to Paul about that. I scolded him for neglecting you too. I told him he needed to take better care of you or he'd wind up losing you to some mysterious stranger." She was joking of course but obviously it wasn't making me feel better.

"Paul promised the two of you would be there, so it's all set. I can't wait to have you meet Warren. You're going to love him," she said.

"I'm sure I will," I told her cheerfully but inside, I was annoyed.

I was annoyed at myself for not being a better friend to her. I was annoyed at myself for not being completely honest with either my supposed fiance or my boyfriend. I was annoyed that they weren't the same person. I was annoyed at Paul for saying we'd be there without asking me. I was unhappy with everything and unsure of how to fix it.

⌘⌘⌘⌘⌘

Friday night at the Bowl-O-Drome, I bowled my first strike. I'd been steadily improving in the bowling department, although better still wasn't necessarily good. I continued to worry about being a disappointing teammate. No one had complained of course, but I fretted nonetheless.

The bowling league finals were coming up and Gus assured me that my strike would help our team in the standings. Gus had originally told me the league bowled until mid-winter, took a break, then started up again. Would they want me to come back? Gus' sister had given birth to her baby and surely Dale's sister's wrist was mending.

Gus and I had been seeing each other every Sunday since our 'real date'. Now that I had my own phone line, we were talking during the week, too but neither of had shown each other much affection at the Bowl-O-Drome. We had never talked about it. We just seemed to have an unspoken agreement that it wasn't the best venue to have everyone know we were more than just friends. I think Maryann knew anyway. She didn't seem to miss a thing although she kept her own counsel.

When I finally bowled the strike, Gus grabbed me and gave me a huge sloppy kiss. I felt my face grow warm with embarrassment or maybe it was just the thrill of the strike and the kiss. Nobody else seemed worried about it at all.

⌘⌘⌘⌘⌘

The next night, was my double date with Paul and Rosemary and Warren. Gus worked at the garage from 7am to 7pm on Saturdays, so he was always really tired by Saturday nights. Our days were Fridays and Sundays. I marveled at how effectively that had worked out for me. It was a dangerous thing. It made me feel like I might be able to make the whole double life thing actually work.

Warren was everything Rosemary had said he was. She was obviously besotted with him. They were affectionate with one another and it was clear the feeling was mutual on his part. Paul was charming and more reserved than the last time I'd seen him. Apparently he didn't consider his excitement over his political future to be proper double date fodder. It was clearly Rosemary's night and he was letting her have it.

I was relieved, in a way, but in a way, I wanted him to be not quite so nice. When I'd seen him last, I'd been angry because he'd made assumptions about our future without my input. Granted, he'd been making those assumptions for years. I'd always just gone along with them. My lack of any previous complaint was just a sign of my tacit approval. Aside from some extra work and some new found excitement about the future, he hadn't changed that much had he?

I had though. My imaginary better version of myself might have deserved nice Paul. The version I actually was, liked it better when she could be angry at him. It was easier.

"I've been in love with Rosemary for years," Warren confided, as we sat down to dinner. "We took ballroom dancing lessons together when we were nine but she's only just noticed me," he added good-naturedly.

"You didn't actually *talk* to me until the night of my debut," she said laughing.

"Well, it took me from age nine, to just a couple of months ago, to get my courage up," he said and they both dissolved into laughter. This was clearly a conversation they'd had before. In the brief time they'd been together it had become part of the fabric of their relationship.

I remembered my own attempts at ballroom dancing lessons. My parents, of course, were convinced that dance lessons were essential for any well-bred young lady. They couldn't have known then, that I would flat out refuse to have a debut and would probably never need to know how to dance.

I had struggled. I had stepped on my partner's feet. He had to keep reminding me that he was supposed to be leading. I told my parents that if I had to learn to dance, what I really wanted, was to learn tap dancing or the hula like they did in the new state of Hawaii. My parents had vetoed both of those ideas in short order.

Rosemary and Warren were both people who could carry a conversation and make you feel as though you were participating even if you really weren't. I was grateful for this. Because of them, it was a nice evening.

Paul drove me home. When we got to my circular driveway I said,

"She seems really happy. Warren is very nice," I added generically. These statements were true albeit vague. I wanted to comment on the evening but I didn't want to be dragged into a serious discussion about other things.

"I think they'll end up getting married," Paul said. Then he gave me a funny look. "Are *you* happy Eleanor?"

So much for no serious discussions about other things. I was caught off guard. Paul and I had never spent any real time discussing our emotions.

"I don't know," I said honestly. It was a relief. It was the first, truly honest thing I'd said to him in months.

He leaned over and kissed me. It was more than a peck and it surprised the heck out of me. But it felt like he was trying too hard. When Gus kissed me it was easy. When Paul kissed me it was like when you try to force the wrong piece into a puzzle; at first glance, it seems like it should fit but now matter how you turn it, it just doesn't work.

"Okay," he said suddenly, pulling away. "Okay," he repeated. "Good night Eleanor."

I didn't know if he meant it was okay if I didn't know I was happy or okay that he'd kissed me awkwardly or if he was okaying some private thought of his own which I wasn't privy to.

⌘⌘⌘⌘⌘

Mike Flanagan didn't show up at work that Monday. There were many times when he was off working on a story but eventually, he was always back in his office pacing around and talking on the phone. At lunchtime, I still hadn't seen him.

"Where's Mike today?" I asked Richard.

"I don't know," he responded. Then said, "Oh wait, I think he said something last week about a doctor's appointment, Maybe that was today. Did you need some help with something?"

Richard had been really awesome at helping me out. Despite being busy with his own stories and continuing to be exhausted by his twins, he was always willing to explain something to me. I sincerely thanked him every time he helped me. I hoped I was expressing my gratitude well enough.

"No, I'm actually fairly self-sufficient today," I said with a laugh. "I just don't usually go a whole day without seeing him, that's all."

"Think of it as a tiny vacation," Richard joked, "I'm sure he'll be back to torturing us all tomorrow."

Snow was falling lightly on my way home. I couldn't believe it was almost Christmas. When you're a little kid, the weeks between Halloween and Christmas seemed like they were interminable, They went on forever. Somehow, when you got to be an adult that time went by incredibly quickly. I wondered if the snow would accumulate much. Gus and I hoped to visit the mystery cave one more time before winter really set in. The mystery cave still resonated with me on some level I didn't really understand.

When I got home, my father asked if the car gave me any trouble in the snow. He hadn't asked about the car in a while.

"I didn't skid at all," I said. Gus had insisted that I let him put new tires on it. That probably had a lot to do with my lack of skidding.

"Good," my father said "Perhaps it's more reliable than I'd feared," he allowed. "It still looks like hell though."

⌘⌘⌘⌘⌘

There was a small park, on my way to work. In the mornings it was usually empty, although if I left Liberty News during the day, it was often populated with mothers and young children. Later in day, on nice afternoons, old men sat on the benches and fed the birds or played checkers.

The next morning, on my way to work, the park was full of people. Most of them appeared to be around my age. I thought maybe they were college students. I was intrigued. I slowed down the Nash to see what was going on. A handwritten banner, strung along a park bench, proclaimed "Join the Peace Corps." I had to swerve to avoid a parked car.

Up to then, Mike had assigned all my stories. I knew though, that other, more experienced reporters, like Richard, also sought out their own stories.

"Pay attention," Richard had told me after Mike promoted me. "Wherever you are, just be alert. News is really just what's happening. If you happen to be there when it's happening, you're going to be the reporter who gets the scoop and Mike will love you forever. Just write your notes and get your story. There's no guarantee Mike will run it but there's a pretty good chance he will."

The twin allure of getting a story all on my own and learning more about the Peace Corps was just too much to turn down. I looked around for a pay phone but couldn't find one. I looked back toward the students in the park. "Be there when it's happening," Richard had told me. If I spent too much time trying to call Liberty News to explain why I was going to be late, I might miss my story entirely. All right, I decided, I'll just have to be late.

I walked back to the park. It was cold out and everyone was bundled up. The weather hadn't seemed to put a damper on the crowd's enthusiasm. Some students were just happy to have an excuse to take a break from their classes but others seemed genuinely interested.

A heavy-set, man with a beard stood holding a microphone. The microphone didn't have very good range and I had to push up through the other students to actually hear what he was saying.

"…and three of my classmates have signed up for the President's Peace Corps. So, that's four of us but we're hoping to get a group of ten together. Who else wants to go?"

One or two hands went up in the crowd.

"Great, great," the bearded man said. "We have some paperwork…" and his microphone cut out. A couple of guys behind him stepped forward and moved some cords and wires. The bearded man tried again. His lips moved but we couldn't hear him. He shook his head. Finally, they got the microphone working. The crowd cheered.

"We have some applications on that table over there," he said, pointing to a wobbly-looking card table. It was breezy and someone had placed a large rock on top of the stack of papers, so they wouldn't blow away.

The bearded man fiddled with the microphone, which had clearly gone out again. He helplessly handed it over to one of the guys behind him. He cupped his hands and yelled.
"Look, I can only yell so much, so if you have questions, come

up and talk to us and we'll try to talk you into the Peace Corps!"

A handful of people went to talk to the bearded man and his classmates. Everyone else drifted away, the main excitement clearly being over. I moved to talk to the bearded man. He talked to a couple of other people before he turned to me.

"So are you interested in joining the Peace Corps?" he asked, looking me over.

"Yes," I admitted, "but right now I'd actually just like to write a story about your and your friends who are joining."

"Story?" he asked. "Are you writing a book?"

"No, I'm a reporter," I said. I hadn't had that many opportunities to say it. It felt great to say it. I didn't know if I would ever get tired of saying it. Saying "I'm Mrs. Putnam and I've organized the charity benefit," was never going to feel anywhere near as good, I decided.

"I work for Liberty News," I added. "So what made you want to join the Peace Corps?"

"Wow! That's really weird," the bearded man said ignoring my question.

"What is?" I asked, genuinely perplexed.

"Liberty News is kind of how I found the Peace Corps."

"I'm sorry," I said. "I'm still not following you."

"Most of my med school classmates are totally caught up in the money aspect of medicine. Except these guys, of course," he gestured towards his other three classmates who were each talking to people from the crowd of students.

"I was thinking about dropping out. I was so discouraged, you know? Do you know what's it's like to feel really different from everybody else in your group?"

"Yes. I really do," I said fighting a sense of déjà vu. Why did this sound so familiar to me?

"Anyway," he went on, "I decided to write to that crazy advice lady at Liberty News. What's her name, Helpful Hilda or something?"

"Harriet," I mumbled with growing realization.

"Yeah, her," he went on. "Anyway, I just felt like I needed some advice from a stranger. Somebody who'd never met me. Sometime the people who know you best can't give you the best advice. Their lives are just too wrapped up in yours to be unbiased, you know?. Anyhow, the advice lady, whatever her name was, said I should consider the Peace Corps, so here I am."

I goggled at him. I'd written something that had changed the course of somebody's life. And I was getting to hear about it. We did things every day that affected people in ways we never knew about. I was dumbfounded.

"Who actually writes that advice column anyway?" he asked. "Is her name actually Harriet?"

"No. It's Candy-somebody-or-other," I answered honestly. I debated telling him it had been me. But it seemed wrong to share that. The moment felt so surreal, it was like a fragile soap bubble. Admitting I'd given the advice felt like it would break that bubble and make the moment somehow less special.

"Well it was good advice, anyway," he said enthusiastically. "I feel like I might be able to make a difference now."

I was glad he chose not to pursue Helpful Harriet's real identity. I talked to the bearded man and his classmates for another 45 minutes, taking notes the whole time.

"If you decide to sign up, they could probably use writers for something," he said, as I was leaving. "I'm not sure exactly what you could do but you could check."

I thanked him again for the interview and told him I'd look into it.

When I finally got to Liberty News it was almost 11am and my fingers were like ice. I figured I might have to hold a mug of that horrible coffee, just to warm them up enough to be able to type my story.

Mike found me before I'd even gotten my coat off.

"You're really late, kid."

"I know and I'm sorry," I said. "But I got a story."

That peaked his interest. His demeanor changed from annoyed to excited as I told him about the impromptu rally in the park.

"Were there any other reporters there?" he asked.

I told him I didn't think so. Only a handful of people had stayed to talk to the Peace Corps volunteers and I hadn't seen anyone taking notes but me.

"Great, kid. The Times has been writing about the Peace Corps for months. All we've managed to get were press releases. I want two stories - a short one about the rally itself and a longer piece about the people who are actually going."

"Thanks, Mike," I said. Stopping at the park had seemed like a fabulous idea when I first had it. But after I left the park and I had finished my drive to Liberty News, doubt had crept in. I was afraid he might say I'd wasted my time on a lousy idea.

"Don't thank me. It's your story."

I stood there for another minute just being astonished by how well it had gone.

"Don't you have words to write?" he asked. "Scram. I'm running it tomorrow, so I need your copy on my desk tonight before you leave."

⌘⌘⌘⌘⌘

Gus was the only person I told about Helpful Harriet and the bearded man.

"Isn't it a strange coincidence, that I ended up talking to the man I helped?' I asked.

"Maybe. Maybe not," Gus told me. "Lots of times, things happen for a reason. I think most of the time there are no coincidences. Things happen, when they do, because that's how it's all supposed to unfold. It's like there's a cosmic plan.. Was it a coincidence that your car broke down at the Bowl-O-Drome or was that supposed to happen so we'd meet?"

"So you think everything is planned out for us by God or the universe?" I asked, genuinely curious. "Do we have any choices?"

"We always have choices," he insisted. "We chose how we behave and how we treat other people and those things really matter. The future is never set in stone. But I do think some things are just meant to be."

I thought about this. For a long time, I never questioned how things were in my life. Then, I started to do things differently than everyone expected. Most of all, I had started to do things differently than *I* expected. There was a certain sense of security in playing by the rules. When you did what was expected of you, it was a safe bet you were doing the right things. Those things might not ultimately make you happy but they probably weren't going to get you into trouble either.

When you started to do things you hadn't even expected from yourself, that seemed a little more dangerous.

"How do we know we're making the right choices?" I asked Gus.

"We don't," he said simply. "We make the best choices we can at the time. Sometimes they're good solid choices that benefit us.

Sometimes we have what seems like a good idea but it turns out dopey. That's the thing with choice. It's kind of a double-edged sword. We have the ability to do great things. We also have the ability to screw things up. But don't worry," he said taking my hand.

His typical grin was back and I was glad to see it.

"You made good choices here. You helped a man find his calling and you got a great story, so don't worry," he repeated. "Plus," he added "I think you did the right thing by not telling him you were Helpful Harriet. Sometimes we can get great advice from stranger."

I was amazed at how he had said essentially the same thing the bearded-man had said. Gus always amazed me in that way. I hoped all my choices would be so good.

⌘⌘⌘⌘⌘

My parents and I frequently went skiing in the mountains for Christmas instead of staying home because we didn't really have any extended family. In a way it was good. Christmas always seemed less lonely than Thanksgiving. Unfortunately, I had never really liked skiing. I liked sitting in the lodge, drinking hot chocolate and watching people but I didn't much care about the skiing itself. Before I got my job and met Gus, it never would have occurred to me to tell my parents I didn't want to go. Things had changed though.

"I don't want to go to the mountains for Christmas," I informed my parents a week before the holiday.

"But dear, we can't cancel our reservations, now," my mother complained. "You want us to stay home?" she asked plaintively. My mother loved her sameness. She believed change should be avoided at all costs.

"I don't want *you* to stay home," I clarified. "I think you and Daddy should go and have a wonderful time."

"You want to stay home *alone*?" she asked horrified. "What about gifts?" she insisted.

Paul and Rosemary always had piles of presents under their family tree. Rosemary once told me it took them hours to open them all on Christmas morning. My parents were far less extravagant in their gift giving. There were a few small, practical gifts and maybe one or two more that they considered frivolous. I was totally okay with their gift giving practices. I never pined for more. I didn't feel I needed a lot of things. But it wasn't like gift giving took up a huge chunk of our holiday either.

"We could exchange gifts before you go or after you come back," I suggested.

My mother looked unconvinced. Surprisingly, my father came to my rescue.

"I think she can stay alone for a couple of days," he told my mother "She's never really liked skiing anyway."

"You haven't?" my mother asked me. "Really?" She had never been as perceptive as my dad was. Mike Flanagan, Richard Noseworthy and Gus all had that gift of really reading people well. I supposed part of why I admired that trait in them was that I also admired it in my father. I hoped I was cultivating it in myself too but I wasn't sure.

"Not really, no." I told her.

"Won't you be lonely?" she asked in a final attempt to try to win me back.

"No, Mother. I'll be fine. Really."

I didn't tell either of my parents that I wouldn't be lonely because while I didn't want to go skiing, I also wasn't going to be spending Christmas alone.

Gus had asked me to come to his house for the day. I had met his mother and cousin of course but all of his sisters and their families were going to be there for Christmas. The sister I had ultimately replaced on the bowling team would be there with her husband and new baby. I was nervous about meeting them all but I knew it was too important to Gus to say no. If my parents had demanded that I go skiing it might have gotten ugly.

⌘⌘⌘⌘⌘

I ended up exchanging gifts with my parents before they left for the mountains. My mother, eternally hopeful that I'd develop some ladylike interests, bought me two new dresses and a pair of pumps which went with both.

My mother had very good taste and a talent for knowing what would look nice on someone else. I was probably never going to have either. I barely knew when *I* looked decent in something, no less when somebody else did. The dresses were pretty. I didn't necessarily feel the urge to shop for more or God forbid, plan a debut, but at least I'd have something nice to wear when I met Gus' family.

My father spent more money than I was used to having him spend. He bought me an electric typewriter. At first, I thought he had found out about my job and was somehow gifting me the typewriter as a way of stating his approval. But then he said,

"Since you're going to secretarial school and learning to type and things, I thought this would be helpful to you when you help with Paul's campaigns."

I was disappointed by his motivation. Why did everyone think running Paul's political campaigns was my great dream in life? But I was actually thrilled with the gift itself, even if I didn't feel I could tell my father why.

⌘⌘⌘⌘⌘

When Gus had first asked me to come for Christmas, I figured it would only be the actual day of Christmas. He soon disabused me of that idea.

"Oh no," he said. "This is the first time all of my sisters have been home at the same time since my dad died. My mother has plans for Christmas Eve, Christmas Day and Boxing Day! You don't want to go back to your empty house alone every night, do you?"

I really didn't but I was unsure if his family would want me there for an entire three days. My family was very self-contained. Especially on the holidays when no one else was around. My parents threw their share of dinner parties throughout the year. Occasionally, they'd host a barbeque during the summer but any holiday had always just been the three of us. I couldn't ever remember them inviting any other person to our house on a holiday.

"Will they really want me there for all that time?" I asked. "I mean, I'm not part of the family or anything."

"Well not yet anyway,' he said flashing the trademark Gus grin. I couldn't tell if he was teasing or serious about that and I was scared to ask.

"Look," he said, "Family are the people who care about you. Sure, some of them are related to you but some are also friends or neighbors or people you just manage to collect on life's journey. It's all relative," he added and laughed out loud at his wordplay.

I had to laugh too. I wondered if he realized that his humor was always contagious for me. Any time I was feeling anxious, he made sure I caught it. I didn't know if he did it consciously or not.

My parents left on Christmas Eve in the morning. Gus picked me up in the afternoon. I had finally agreed to let him pick me up at home instead of meeting him at the Bowl-O-Drome. I still didn't really want him to see my house but I also knew it was important to him to let him pick me up. At least he wasn't going to awkwardly bump into my parents.

"Big house," was all he said when I got into the car.

"It's too big," I said.

"Oh, you'll probably be desperate for more room by the day after tomorrow," he teased. "My house isn't nearly so big as yours but my mother is going to fill it with all kinds of people."

His house was smaller than mine but it was lit up with Christmas lights and smelled like heaven. Decorating for Christmas was one of those things my parents always considered overindulgent. A simple wreath hung on our front door. A small tree stood in our living room with a few ornaments which were all the same size and all red and gold. The single strand of lights was white.

Gus' house was a riot of color both inside and out. Christmas cards of all shapes and sizes had been taped around the kitchen door frame. Christmas decorations sat on every available surface. Painted macaroni treasures clearly made by school kids sat next what looked like family heirloom antiques. Obviously, each was considered valuable.

Maryann, who'd always been somewhat reserved toward me at the bowling alley, enfolded me into a giant hug. She was in her element here at her own house and Christmas was obviously her thing.

"We're really happy to have you here, Eleanor," she said.

"I'm happy to be here," I told and her and I was, even though I was also nervous.

I wanted to offer to help her in some way but Gus was dragging me off before I could. Maryann, called after us,

"See if you can find Elizabeth. She's supposed to do something with these potatoes."

The house was completely filled with people. I tried to yank off my sweater as we walked. I was really warm. Gus held my hand. He had a greeting for every person we encountered. In the first ten minutes I'd been there, he'd introduced me to at least a dozen people. I wished we all had name tags. I feared I was going to forget someone's name and end up offending them.

Finally, we found Gus' sister, Liz. She was the sister who was closest to him in age. She looked like him too with dark hair and dark eyes. She was holding a baby who was looking around. I wasn't sure how much babies could see. I remembered learning at school, that babies couldn't see that far at first.

Her face lit up when she saw Gus. She hugged him awkwardly while she continued to hold the baby. The baby wasn't sure he appreciated being jostled and began to cry a little. Liz made soothing noises and managed to settle him back down. Then she hugged me and set him off again.

"Give me my nephew," he said, taking the baby from her like he'd been holding babies his whole life. Maybe he had, for all I knew. He was different here, somehow. He was still Gus, obviously. He was still attentive and affectionate toward me but this was his family. Everyone here knew him and loved him. He was easygoing everywhere but it was like he was at his maximum comfort level here. I wished I felt more comfortable here. I didn't even achieve his level of ease with my own family.

Gus was making goofy faces at the baby and bouncing him up and down a little.

"He just ate, not too long ago," Liz warned. "Don't jiggle him too much or you'll be sorry," she laughed.

"Mom said you're supposed to go do something with potatoes," he commanded and he laughed too.

Liz kissed the baby on his head, then kissed Gus in the exact same way. She favored me with an amazing smile and went to find her mother in the kitchen. This family had a lock on smiling. They were good at it. They did it all the time and they did it with their entire face. Did my family ever smile at all? Well occasionally, I admitted to myself but not like this.

An elderly couple got up off the couch and walked toward another part of the house. Gus motioned that we should sit down. I was happy to. I was feeling a little overwhelmed.

I smiled at the baby and he smiled back. Even the babies in this family were good smilers!

"What's his name?" I asked.

'Matthew," he said. "Do you want to hold him?"

I was taken aback. In eighteen years, I had never actually held a baby before. I said as much.

"Really?" he asked surprised. "Never?"

"Never," I admitted.

"Well once they can hold their heads up on their own, like this guy, they don't quite seem so fragile anymore."

"I don't know…" I began but Gus was already settling Matthew into my lap. He moved my arms, so the baby wasn't in any danger of toppling off my lap or the couch. He was incredibly warm and heavier than I thought he'd be. The top of his head smelled nice.

"Hello," I said to him in wonder.

He reached up and grabbed small fistful of my hair. Gus had to untangle us but I kept holding him. Holding a baby wasn't really such a scary thing. People all around the world had been doing it every single day for thousands of years. I felt the same sense of connectedness holding him that I'd felt at the mystery cave. I wasn't just an isolated lonely being slowly circling around other isolated lonely beings. I was part of something bigger. By the time Liz came back to retrieve Matthew, I was no longer nervous about holding him. I was actually sorry to let him go.

⌘⌘⌘⌘⌘

It turned out, that not everyone who was in the house, was staying overnight. By 11pm a lot of people had gone home. Most would be back at some point in the next couple of days. I was hoping to get to hold Matthew again but Liz was one of the people who went home. Her husband Bill was a night watchman somewhere and he'd had to work on Christmas Eve. She assured her mother that she'd be back with both Bill and Matthew early the next morning. Matthew was sound asleep on her shoulder when she left.

"Sure, he's zonked out now," she said with a quiet laugh, "But he won't stay like this all night. Not yet, anyway. He'll be awake, squalling and starving before we even get home.

I was also hoping for a chance to get to know Gus' two older sisters better. Unfortunately, by the time everyone who was leaving, had left, I wasn't much more alert than the baby had been. Before I knew it, Gus was gently shaking me awake. My neck was stiff from falling asleep on his shoulder.

Maryann handed him a blanket and a pillow and he installed me on the sofa in the tiny den down the hall from the living room. Neither he nor his sisters seemed tired at all. He leaned over and kissed me on the forehead. I had the overwhelming sensation of being a little kid again. I was too tired to feel any indignity in it.

"Sleep," he whispered. "I'll come check on you before I go to bed and make sure you don't need anything. The Montovani clan gets up pretty early on Christmas morning," he warned. "Sleep," he repeated. I did.

⌘⌘⌘⌘⌘

I was dreaming the Peace Corps dream again. Paul had said I shouldn't go. He'd been angry and said it wasn't going to help his political career. He asked why I wanted to do it if it wasn't going to help him. But then I was in Africa anyway and Gus was holding my hand. Someone in the village was playing a strange musical instrument. It was really loud.

I blinked a few times, realizing I was awake now but not entirely sure where I was. I remembered, after a few seconds but the noise from my dream persisted. I wrapped my bathrobe around myself and went to go see what was going on.

The noise turned out to be an accordion Gus turned out to be playing it. Everyone looked tremendously happy about it. I wondered if I was still dreaming. My dream had actually made more sense. At least I had context for my Peace Corps longings. Gus playing Christmas carols on the accordion was just bizarre.

When he saw me, he finished his song with a flourish and put the instrument down. He gave me a big hug.

"What's with the accordion?" I asked softly.

"Long story," he explained. "I'll tell you all about it later."

There were a lot fewer people in the house on Christmas morning than there had been on Christmas Eve but there were still a lot more people than I was used to. Liz had returned as promised with her husband and a smiling Matthew. Gus' other sisters Barbara and Carmen were each there with a husband and two kids. There were fourteen of us all together.

The kids were all anxious to open presents but Maryann insisted that everyone eat breakfast first. She assigned everybody a task. Gus was scrambling eggs on the stove. I remembered the first night I'd met him at the Bowl-O-Drome, he had said he was good at cooking eggs. I was at the opposite end of the kitchen feeding slices of bread into the toaster. A tall man with a cowboy hat came over with butter, jelly and a knife in his hand.

"I come from a small family myself," he said in a Texas drawl. "This," he gestured around the kitchen, "took a little gettin' used to. I'm John," he added "Barbara's husband."

"I'm Eleanor," I said extending my hand. He enfolded it in his huge one. "My family is small too," I confided in him. "They're not anything like this. Not that this is bad," I added hurriedly lest he take offense.

But he remained jovial.

"Not bad, darlin', just really, really loud."

After we'd eaten breakfast, we all sat in the living room. I finally got to sit next to Gus. We sat together on the floor with the kids. Presents spilled out from under the tree. I wondered briefly if my parents were having a nice time in the mountains.

To my surprise, there were a couple of different packages for me. I had brought a bottle of wine and handed it to Maryann when I'd arrived the night before. I had no idea if anyone in the family even drank wine but it seemed like an appropriate gift to bring when you're invited to somebody's house for a few days.

I had bought Gus a cashmere scarf. As I'd been leaving the department store with the scarf, I walked by a table with books about the constellations. The books were really aimed at kids but the pictures were beautiful. I bought the book for him too. I remembered that he'd talked about the stars when we'd gone to the mystery cave. Now I was afraid the scarf would seem too impersonal and the book too silly.

I sat with my own gifts in my lap, still wrapped.

"Are you going to open those?" Gus asked. "Or just hang onto them until next Christmas?"

"I like to watch people's faces as they open theirs," I said. "I can't do that if I'm opening mine. I actually wish I'd brought more for everyone," I said worriedly.

"You did fine,' Gus said. "I didn't even tell you about everyone who would be here."

Then, Maryann also asked me if I was going to open my presents. I didn't want to hurt anyone's feelings or seem ungrateful in any way.

"Open mine first," Gus demanded. His eyes shining. He was just as excited as the kids were. He plucked one of the boxes out of my lap and handed it to me. Under the wrapping paper was a long black box. Nestled on top of a fluffy bit of cotton was a fine silver chain. An elaborate filigreed letter "E" dangled from the chain. It was beautiful. Gus hooked the clasp around my neck. I was glad he did, because all of the sudden my fingers seemed shaky.

"The other one is from me," Maryann said .

The second package contained a matching bracelet. A smaller, filigreed letter "E" hung like a charm form the bracelet. Gus helped me put that one on too.

"I'm glad you decided to bowl with us," Maryann said.

"Me too," Gus said.

"Me too," I added.

Family, friends and neighbors were in and out all day. Maryann set food out on a long table like a buffet. We didn't have a sit down meal but people could pick at food throughout the day. I talked to all kinds of people. I was glad I actually had things to talk about. A year before, I don't think I would have been able to make anything interesting come out of my mouth. Of course, a year before, I never would have had the opportunity to talk to so many people.

Late in the afternoon, Gus said, "Grab your coat. We're going to go outside for a while."

He wore the scarf I'd given him. At least it was a useful gift.

It was so warm in the house, outside seemed colder than it actually was. His neighborhood was quiet and the sun was beginning to go down.

"I love this time of day," he told me. "The light makes everything look all golden. The edges of everything sort of blur and everything seems softer in some way."

"It is pretty," I murmured. I'd always felt the same way he did about the late afternoons but I'd never articulated it in quite that way.

"So what are we doing out here?" I asked.

"You're not too cold, are you?" he asked, concerned. "I mean, I have this warm scarf some great girl got me, so I'm fine," he said flipping the end of said scarf dramatically over his shoulder.

"You really like it?" I asked, feeling suddenly insecure. "And the book too?"

"Of course I like them," he reassured me. "I like *you*. And you gave them to me, so they're great."

"I like you too and I'm not cold but really, where are we going?"

"We're just taking a little walk," he said, squeezing my hand. "I got tired of sharing you with my family."

"I like your family," I said. "Sometimes, I don't feel like I belong in mine," I added.

"How come?" he asked.

I realized, too late, that I was treading on potentially dangerous ground. I had told Gus almost nothing about my family. It wasn't that I was embarrassed by them or by him either for that matter. It was more than just having secrets. It went back to the person I had always been and the person I seemed to be becoming How was I ever going to reconcile those two?

I decided I might be safe in telling him some of it anyway.

"Remember when my friend had her debut? I had to re-schedule our first date, so I could go to the party?" Had that really only been three months ago?

"Sure, I remember," he said. "You went flying out of the Bowl-O-Drome in that crazy, fancy dress."

I blushed a little. I hadn't realized he'd seen me after I'd changed in the Bowl-O-Drome's bathroom.

"Remember how you asked me if that was what I wanted?" I asked.

'Yes," he said cautiously.

"Well it wasn't what I wanted and it still isn't. But it is something my parents want very much for me."

Once I started to talk about it, it got easier. I told him about the broken arm and the vet and the growing gap between what I wanted for myself and what my parents thought I should be. I even told him there was someone my parents assumed I'd marry. I just didn't say I'd had those assumptions myself until just recently.

He was quiet for a while after I finished. We continued to walk.

"It can be difficult," he said, finally. "To make choices for ourselves when people who care about us want something different. That whole scene with the accordion this morning? My dad used to play. The Christmas morning thing was his bit. He taught me how to play but it was never my favorite instrument. I play sometimes, because my mom wants me to."

"So we should do everything our parents' ask of us?" I asked.

"God, no," he said emphatically. "It's important to stand up for yourself and to be yourself. Nobody else can live your life for you, no matter how good their intentions. The thing is, to find a balance. If it's really a matter of your you-ness..."

"You-ness?" I interrupted. "What's you-ness?"

"You know, all those things that make you, you," he explained. "So, if it's really a matter or your you-ness," he continued, "then you should stick to your guns. So, I think you're right, in not doing a debut. It sounds like you've felt that way for a long time. For me, the accordion is not my first choice but playing a few songs on Christmas doesn't compromise my soul in any way."

We were both quiet for a while after that but I could feel there was more he wanted to say.

At last, he said, "It may not be any of my business but do your parents know you don't want to marry the guy they had in mind.?"

"Not yet," I said.

"You should probably tell them," he suggested with a little edge to his voice.

"I will," I assured him a little defensively. I wanted to tell him it was so much more complicated than that. But was it complications or cowardice that kept me keeping secrets?

"It's getting dark," he said "We should get back."

⌘⌘⌘⌘⌘

That night, Christmas night, I managed to stay awake. I had talked to Liz for a little while the night before but I finally managed to talk to Gus' other sisters. Barbara had met John and moved to Texas. They owned a small ranch and raised cattle. I thought briefly of my predecessor as Happy Harriet and her moving to breed horses. I wondered how that was working out for her.

Gus' sister, Carmen, had moved to California to become a movie star. Acting hadn't worked out too well for her but she'd met her husband, Bob and they'd ended up starting a successful charter fishing boat company.

Everyone in Gus' family was super nice to me. I was glad he'd invited me. We talked long into the night.

The next day I found myself leaning on the windowsill watching Gus play kickball with his older nieces and nephews. He'd asked if I wanted to join them but I hadn't really packed the right shoes for kickball. I was disappointed. It looked like they were having a great time. I absently fidgeted with the silver "E" dangling from my neck.

The house was quieter than it had been in two days. Gus' sisters and their families were leaving that night or the next morning. I was due to go home myself that night. My parents were coming home sometime the next afternoon.

Maryann came up behind me and startled me a little.

"Sorry," she apologized. "I didn't mean to scare you."

"It's okay," I told her. "He's great with the kids," I said, nodding towards Gus and the kickball game. I moved over so she could stand next to me at the windowsill.

"He is." she said. "He'll be a good dad someday. Just like his own dad," she added wistfully.

She was quiet for a few moments. I felt bad. I hoped I hadn't made her sad. From what Gus had said, the whole family had really struggled with his father's loss.

When she finally spoke again though, she didn't bring up Gus' father.

"Have you decided yet?" she asked me.

I turned so I could really look at her. She always looked as though she knew exactly what was in my head although we seldom made more than polite conversation at the Bowl-O-Drome. I was confused.

"I'm sorry, what?' I asked.

"Have you decided?" she asked again. "You can't live in two different worlds, you know. You can live in one and visit the other. I think you've done that quite nicely so far but in the end, you need to choose which one you're actually going to make a life in. The lucky thing is that usually you get to make the choice about which one you belong in but eventually you do have to decide."

How was it that all of the sudden my life was filled with perceptive people? How was I was so transparent to everyone else when I'd barely even figured things out myself? I didn't even know how to answer her.

"I'm sorry," she said genuinely. "I didn't mean to put you on the spot or make you uncomfortable. I just hope you'll think about it."

I promised her I would. I didn't know what else to say. I'd already thought about it quite a bit and hadn't been able to come up with any resolution.

Gus brought me home a few hours later. The moon was rising on the drive home. It was huge and yellow and looked close enough to touch.

"Thanks for spending Christmas with me," Gus said pulling me in for a kiss after he stopped the car.

"I had a nice time," I said.

I grabbed my key from my purse and got out of the car .

"I'll stay until you get into the house and get the lights on," Gus said.

"Thanks," I said.

"Your parents will be home tomorrow? You'll be okay tonight on your own?" he asked concerned.

"Sure," I said. "I'm pretty tired anyway. I'll probably just go to sleep."

I waved to him from the doorway so he knew I was all set.

"Hey Ellie?" he called from the car.

"Yeah?" I asked, hesitating in the doorway.

"I love you!" he yelled out the open car window, then pulled out of the driveway before I could even respond.

I didn't get much sleep after all.

⌘⌘⌘⌘⌘

I had enjoyed meeting Gus' family but I'd had three days off
and I actually missed Liberty News. I knew people who had to
drag themselves to work every day. They had bad bosses or
tedious jobs. Going to work was a chore. I didn't know if it was
because I really liked what I was doing or because I felt like
having my job was a privilege but I had missed being at work.

I went to find Mike to see what he had for assignments for me.
He was in his office, just sitting at his desk. Normally, he was on
the phone and pacing or just pacing. It was a surprise to see him
sitting still. I knocked n his door and he motioned for me to come
in. More surprising than his sitting still, was his appearance. He
looked awful. Dark circles rimmed his eyes. He looked
impossibly tired.

"Are you okay?" I asked him.

"I'm fine, kid," he said. At least his voice sounded like his own.
"I hate the holidays. I always wind up with some goddamned head
cold."

It didn't look like he had a head cold but I wasn't going to argue
with him about it. Still, I was concerned. I talked to Richard after
lunch.

"How was your Christmas?" I asked

"It's weird," he mused. "I am now Santa Claus. How did that
happen? Although," he added, "the twins were still more
interested in boxes and bows than the actual presents." He smiled.

"Is Mike okay?" I asked him. "He doesn't look well."

"He always gets sick over the holidays," Richard confided.

"That's what he said too," I said.

"Don't worry," Richard advised, "I'm sure he'll be his annoying old self any day now."

⌘⌘⌘⌘⌘

I kept thinking about Maryann's comment about choosing between two worlds. Paul would have said she was presumptuous to have made it in the first place. Not that I'd ever be able to tell him about it. I owed him an honest conversation, at the very least. I owed Gus more honesty than I'd given him too. I owed my parents some apologies for lying. The only place I was truly being authentic was at Liberty News and even there, I was writing under a sort of pseudonym.

I didn't know what was wrong with me. I was pretty sure I knew what I wanted but having it meant giving up something else. Until seven months before I'd never had to make a hard decision. My choices had been about what to wear to school or what food to eat at dinner. None of them really had any long term effect on my life. The choices I made now would become the rest of my life. I was terribly afraid of screwing it up forever.

So, I dragged my feet. I felt bad. I fixed nothing. Nobody got an honest conversation. I don't know how long I might have plodded along like that, except that three things happened at the beginning of the new year which changed everything.

The first thing, was that our bowling team actually made it to the bowling championship. Gus, Dale and Maryann were all decent bowlers to begin with. I had evolved into a decent enough bowler. A team of all Eleanors would not have managed to get to the championship tournament but it turned out that having one of me wasn't a huge liability either.

Gus said, the team hadn't participated in the tournament in several years. The Bowl-O-Drome actually had 32 different teams who bowled at various times. Out of those thirty-two, eight went into the playoffs. One would eventually win a small amount of cash and each team member would get a trophy. I didn't care much about the cash. I surprised myself, though, by really hoping to earn a trophy.

Our spirits were high. We laughed and joked and shoved one

another affectionately. I remembered how I'd envied that physical affection when I'd first seen it. Inexplicably, I'd become part of it. Gus joked that if we won, he was going to ask me to marry him and we laughed some more. We couldn't wait for our tournament to begin.

The second thing that happened, was that Rosemary got engaged. She called me and asked me to come to her house. I sat on her bed, like I had a hundred times before. She showed me her engagement ring and talked about wedding gowns. She was over the moon happy and I was really happy for her.

I was sorry for the distance between us now although she seemed not to notice it. I didn't know if she was distracted by being in love or just being noble but she behaved as she always had with me. I felt like we'd had so much more in common when we were younger. I marveled at Rosemary. She was such a perfect fit for her life. I couldn't imagine her belonging anywhere else but right where she was.

I was supposed to fit into that life too. It had never been a great fit, true, but I always imagined I'd figure out a way to make it work. I was stubborn. Sheer force of will, right? I remembered Paul's awkward kiss. Maybe some things just didn't fit no matter how hard you tried.

"You should come to the bridal shop with me, Eleanor. You can start thinking about your wedding dress too," she said hopefully.

I had only seen Paul once since we'd double-dated with Rosemary and Warren. We continued to talk on the phone occasionally. I knew he was working on another big case at the law firm and that he and his father continued to plan his political future. But it felt like a big gaping hole had opened up between Paul and I.

I couldn't tell him about the things that were really important to me. Frankly, he didn't seem all that interested anyway. He asked only occasional and cursory questions about secretarial school. In a way, it was a blessing, because it meant I didn't have to lie. I'd been doing far too much of that lately. I was glad his political aspirations made him happy but I could see myself fitting in with them less and less.

"I don't know that Paul and I are ready to get married yet," I cautioned her.

"Don't be silly," she advised, "Paul has been working really hard lately but you know he's doing it for you. You know you were meant to be together."

I wasn't sure about either of those things. I didn't think Paul's political hopes had anything to do with me at all and meant to be seemed kind of crazy. Was anything meant to be? I remembered Gus' comments on that. How was it that people like Rosemary and Gus always seemed so sure they were doing the right things? They felt like certain things were supposed to happen and they were able to just go with that. I always felt like I was swimming against the current no matter what I did.

"Paul might just surprise you, one of these days," Rosemary said cryptically. She wouldn't say more. I suspected that Paul surprising me might end badly for everyone at this point.

The third thing that happened was that Mike Flanagan went into the hospital. His doctors said it was something called walking pneumonia. They said he'd been working too hard. The cigarettes he smoked wasn't helping and neither was his drinking.

"Should we go see him?" I asked Richard.

"I went last night, when he called to tell me he was in there. He's really, really cranky," Richard warned. "But," he added, "You can go if you want to. Just make sure you do it after work," he cautioned. "Mike will have a fit, if he thinks we're not working here."

Despite Richard's warnings about Mike's mood, I decided to go to the hospital anyway. Mike was propped up in bed, reading one of the big New York papers.

"Dirty rag," he muttered and tossed it on the tray next to his bed.

"What's up, kid?" he asked, when he saw me. "Richard's not having a problem is he?"

"No, Richard is fine," I said. "I just came to see how you were." Frankly, he looked terrible. He looked worse than he had that day in the office.

"I can't wait to get out of this goddamned place. The food is miserable and I can't smoke."

"Should you be smoking with pneumonia?" I asked.

"Probably not," he said and proceeded to go off on a coughing fit . When the coughing finally tapered off, he leaned back against his pillows. He gave me a weak smile. He was really pale.

"Okay. Definitely not but I don't know if I can quit either."

We were quiet for a few moments. His admission that he wouldn't be able to quit smoking made him seem vulnerable. It made me sad. We made a little bit of small talk. I couldn't tell if he was glad for my company or annoyed by it. After another ten or fifteen minutes, I got up to leave.

"You probably need to rest," I told him.

"I need to get out of this goddamned hospital, kid." But he leaned back on his pillows and closed his eyes as I left. As I walked down the hall I heard him succumb to another coughing fit

⌘⌘⌘⌘⌘

Paul did indeed surprise me by asking me on a date for that Saturday. He was the same as he'd always been and yet he wasn't. He had a hard edge of determination to him. In the past several months I had seen him by turns distracted and enthusiastic. It was almost as if those two states had distilled somehow into what he was now. He was still polished and polite but where those qualities had always just seemed like Paul to me. Now it was like a means to an end.

"I have good news," he announced after the waiter had brought our dinners. I smiled at him, hoping his news would be work-related. No such luck.

"I'm ready for us to get married, Eleanor."

I didn't say anything. The seconds stretched out and still I didn't.

"You look like maybe this isn't good news after all," he said. His tone was just curious. There wasn't any anger in it yet.

"I'm not sure *I'm* ready for us to get married, Paul." It wasn't the entire truth but it was more truth than I'd given him in a long time.

"Why not?' he asked 'Your little secretarial school thing is done next month. What will you even have to do after that?"

I was mildly distressed that he remembered when secretarial school ended. More than that though, I was angry about how he'd referred to it. Even though I'd dropped out a long time before, I felt defensive. Yet when he suggested it originally, we'd both thought it was just a way of killing time. I'd barely communicated with him in the past few months. How was he to know things had changed? This required a different strategy, I realized. Getting mad at him wasn't going to get me anywhere good right now.

"You just took my by surprise," I said and at least that was true. "We've both been really focused on other things," I admitted. " I might just need a little time," I finished.

"Well, finish secretarial school," he said, "then we'll talk about it again. Okay?"

"Okay," I said with a lightness I didn't feel. I was a dope. I knew I didn't want to marry Paul. It didn't matter how much time I had to be ready. But even then I was sure if I just had enough time to think about it, I could work it so no one got hurt or somehow it would magically work itself out. Really, I was only postponing the inevitable at that point. It was all going to fall apart and it wasn't going to be pretty.

⌘⌘⌘⌘⌘

Mike Flanagan came home from the hospital. His doctors said he was well enough to return to work if he took it easy. They apparently didn't know that Mike Flanagan never took it easy. He still looked unwell to me but he sounded like his old self. He seemed relieved to be back to work.

Our bowling team progressed through the finals and to the final championship game.

Gus continued to love me in a way I was certain I didn't deserve.

Paul and I began to go to dinner again on Saturday nights. We hadn't discussed marriage again, instead sticking to safer topics.

Everything proceeded along in life. I felt like a ticking time bomb.

⌘⌘⌘⌘⌘

The Nash had been making unhappy noises again. On the day of the final bowling championship game, it wouldn't start. I had gotten to work that morning and home that afternoon. When I tried to leave for the Bowl-O-Drome, the engine flatly refused to turn over. The car had caused me a lot of trouble but it had brought me to places I wouldn't otherwise have traveled too. This was true both literally and figuratively. Maybe Gus was right and some things were meant to be.

I had to trek back up the lane, sneak back into the house and call Gus to pick me up. My parents were hosting a dinner party. Cars were arriving in the driveway. With luck, his would be just one more and nobody would notice.

Gus, Maryann, Dale and I performed like we'd been bowling together all of our lives. Everything just seemed to go perfectly. Each of us bowled a strike and a couple of spares except Gus. He bowled two strikes and five spares! Winning seemed surreal. I clutched my trophy with the little gold bowler on it like I'd never before held anything so precious. Maybe I hadn't.

Ever since last my marriage conversation with Paul, I'd felt a near constant tightness in my chest. I'd read somewhere that there were snakes in the Amazon called anacondas who squeezed their prey to death. I thought maybe I knew what those people felt like except my squeezing was more emotional than giant snake.

When we won the bowling championship, I felt that feeling ease off a little bit. I felt a little like I had the day Gus and I had watched clouds. I got so used to the tension inside me, I didn't even notice it until it was gone. Gus was in a great mood too as he drove me home.

"I have something to ask you," he said as we pulled into my driveway. Too late I realized that I had meant to ask him to drop me off by the gatehouse where my currently dead car was parked. I had been pretty sure his car wouldn't be noticed as my parents guests were arriving at their dinner party.

It was later now, though and no doubt everyone who was going to be there was there already. A new car pulling into the driveway was going to be suspicious. A lone figure walked out from between two parked cars and was caught momentarily in Gus' headlights. It was Paul.

"Oh, no," I said.

"What?" Gus asked, confused but I was already getting out of the car. He left the engine running and the lights on but put it into park and got out after me.

"Paul," I said helplessly.

"Eleanor," he said in a measured tone. "I came to talk to you. I thought you'd been behaving strangely lately. I was worried. Your parents said you'd gone to bed early. They said that you went to bed early every single Friday night. Apparently they were wrong."

"Ellie?" Gus asked tentatively. "What's going on? Who's this?"

"Yes, *Ellie,*" Paul's voice had a sarcastic note I'd never heard before. "Who is *this*?"

"Paul Phillip Putnam III, this is Giuseppe Leonardo Montovani."

They actually shook hands The absurdity of the whole thing struck me. It might have even been comical if I hadn't been having trouble breathing and didn't feel like my world was imploding.

"I'm her fiance," Paul said with forced brightness. "How do you know our Eleanor?" He put a possessive arm around my shoulder. I tried to step away but he anticipated it and moved with me.

Gus gave me a look that seemed to suck what little oxygen I was getting right out of my lungs.

"I'm her mechanic," he said carefully. "She's had some car trouble and I came to look at it for her."

"Great," said Paul, as if this were the most reasonable thing in the world.

"I'll give you a call in a few days," Gus said flatly. "I'll let you know if you know if I can order that part you need. Good night, *Eleanor.*" He got in is car and drove away. After he left, I realized my bowling trophy was still in his front seat. It seemed too much to bear at that moment that Gus and the trophy were both gone.

⌘⌘⌘⌘⌘

Paul told my parents some story about my having been awake after all. It didn't matter that I had my coat on. It was Paul's story, so they weren't going to be suspicious of it. Paul asked my father if we could sit in his study as we had some things to discuss. He actually gave my father a wink. I was a little bit afraid of this Paul. Paul was usually solid and steady and never got flustered.

This Paul went beyond that. He seemed downright cold and calculating.

My parents continued with their dinner party. Through my father's closed study door, I could still hear laughter and tinkling of glassware. Paul poured two glasses of brandy from the cut crystal decanter on my father's desk. My father would have been totally fine with his familiarity. Paul sipped his brandy. I just fidgeted with my glass.

"So," he began, with that same eerie calmness. "As I said, I've been concerned about you. You haven't seemed like yourself. I got it in my head somehow, that maybe you were being maltreated at secretarial school. I thought perhaps I could help you in some way."

"Did you go there?" I asked. This was the first thing I'd said since we'd ensconced ourselves in my father's study.

"Oh, yes. Imagine my surprise, when they barely even remembered you because you stopped going after the first month."

It had been closer to six weeks but I wasn't about to correct him. Instead, I said "I intend to pay you back for my tuition money."

"I don't really care about that," he said casually. "What I care about, is why you've been lying. I care about why you've been telling me secretarial school is great and you're learning a lot when you haven't been going. I care about why you still drive into the city every day. I care about why your parents think you're in bed when you're out with some guy. What is going on with you, Eleanor? Or should I start calling you *Ellie*? What's that all about?"

I told him about Anita-what's her name and the secretarial school internships. I told him about Liberty News and Helpful Harriet eloping. I told him about the Nash breaking down at the Bowl-O-Drome and how Gus offered to fix it if I joined the bowling team. I told him about Mike Flanagan and the bowling championship.

It was relief to me to tell him the truth. I talked for a long time. He mostly just listened. Occasionally, he'd nod or say I see. I wasn't sure he did. I had hoped he'd be pleased that I'd finally managed some honesty but I couldn't gauge his reaction.

"What about *him!*" he asked and I knew he meant Gus. It turned out that telling the truth was like eating potato chips; once I started with one, I felt I had to keep going.

"I'm in love with him," I said simply.

Paul absorbed this as if it were just a statistic and not an emotional sucker punch.

After a bit he said, "So, this is what we'll do. First of all, you'll stop seeing him. You'll stop hanging around at bowling alleys and you'll sell that ridiculous car. You'll quit your job and you and I will get married this spring just like we planned to. We won't even tell your parents about the secretarial school debacle."

"But Paul…" I protested. "Didn't you hear me? I can't marry you. I love someone else." I was starting to feel desperate here. I tried to keep it out of my voice but it crept in anyway, putting me at a disadvantage.

"Love is largely irrelevant in a marriage," he said dismissively. This was the most shocking thing I'd ever heard him say. "You'll get over some loser you met in a bowling alley." He said the last two words like it was the vilest place he could imagine.

"Go to bed, Eleanor. I'm tired of talking to you tonight." He stormed out across my father's study but he shut the door gently.

I had thought Paul would be patient and reasonable. Sure, I had worried about hurting his feelings but I had been completely blindsided by his anger. Had he always been so controlling? Had I missed that because I'd never thought to be anything but compliant? I had been sure that finally telling the truth would fix everything. I had fixed nothing. I had been dismissed like a naughty child. It didn't seem possible I could have made things worse but I had.

I called Gus that night and no one answered. When I woke up the next morning to my cold open window and goosebumps, I realized he'd be at work at the garage for the entire day. I tried again Saturday night.

"Look," he said. "I'm exhausted and I don't even know what I want to say to you. I'll come see you tomorrow and maybe you can explain things to me."

I told him not to come into the driveway. I told him I'd meet him by the gatehouse.

"Whatever you want," he sighed, defeated.

⌘⌘⌘⌘⌘

On Sunday morning, I walked down the lane in my heavy boots. It had snowed in the last week and now there were three or four inches on the ground. We sat in Gus' car with the engine running and the heater on. I suggested that we go somewhere but he said, "We're fine here."

I wanted to touch him but I was afraid I'd lost that privilege. We each sat as close to our respective doors as we could. The three or four feet of car seat between us seemed like the Grand Canyon.

"You have a fiance," he began.

"Not really," I said. "Well, not officially. Everybody always just assumed we'd get married but I didn't have a ring or anything. He never exactly asked me."

"He seemed to think you were part of that everybody who assumed you'd get married," he said flatly.

"I was once," I said "but that changed."

"When?" he asked.

"When I met you."

"I don't know what's true, Ellie... Eleanor... hell, I don't even know what to call you anymore."

"Either is fine," I said, hoping against hope that he'd chose Ellie. Then, maybe things could go back to being like they were.

"You said you'd never really had a boyfriend, yet you had a fiance. How does that happen? Did you love him?" he asked.

How could I explain that Paul assumed we'd get married, yet we didn't do many things together and we'd barely ever touched. It was absurd but I'd never really noticed the strangeness of it, until I had something entirely different with Gus.

"Not like I love you," I said. It was the first time I'd told him I loved him. I wished I was telling him in a better way. I was talking. I was finally being honest. I still wasn't making things better.

"I care about Paul," I continued. "I love him in a way, I guess, but it's not the same." I was struggling to put my feelings into words.

"So you lied to this Paul guy?" Gus asked. It actually sounded like he had more sympathy for Paul than for me right then.

"Yes. And my parents. And my friend Rosemary. I was supposed to be in secretarial school, then Liberty News offered me a job and I met you and joined your bowling team and I didn't tell any of them any of it. I didn't think they would understand."

"Which parts didn't you think *I'd* understand?" Gus asked.

"The big house, my parent's money...Paul."

" I can't speak for the other people in your life, but I wish you'd have been honest with me. I'm not sure I would have understood either it would have been nice if you'd given me the chance."

"I wish I'd given you that chance too," I said softly.

We sat still and quiet for what seemed like a long time. Tears rolled silently down my cheeks. I didn't bother to wipe them away.

"I wanted to give you this," Gus said finally.

My heart leapt a little. He had been about to ask me something, before everything had fallen apart on Friday night.

He handed me my bowling trophy. "You left this in the car on Friday."

"Thanks," I said. I tried to touch his hand as he handed it to me but he pulled away.

"You should have this too," he said. He handed me a sheaf of papers.

"What is this?" I asked him

"Peace Corps application," he said. "That was your dream, wasn't it? Or did you lie about that too?"

"No," I said sadly. "That was the truth. I may have left some things out," I added, "but I didn't actually ever lie to you." I knew I was in the wrong but I was starting to feel touchy about it. I wanted him to be on my side, even though I'd been the one to hurt him.

"Leaving things out, are just lies of omission. They're still dishonest." We were both quiet again. Part of me wanted to deny that I'd mistreated him but the better part knew he was right.

"You should apply to the Peace Corps. It'll give you time to figure out what you want in life." he said.

"But I know what I want," I protested.

"I'm not sure you do," he said resignedly. "Look, maybe you do love me but you didn't stand up for me and that hurt." He paused to let that sink in. "Do you know what was worse?' he demanded.

"No," I said in a small voice. I couldn't imagine what could be worse.

"You didn't stand up for yourself. You deserve to have the life you want but sometimes you have to fight for that. It doesn't just happen. You claim you love Liberty News and the Bowl-O-Drome and me," he added. "But you were afraid to own up to loving us. You were willing to deny us all and stay with a life somebody else wanted for you. If you join the Peace Corps, maybe you'll learn how to stand up for yourself by standing up for other people."

I sat there feeling like I'd been kicked in the stomach.

"I need to go," Gus said in a choked voice.

"Okay," I said, even though it wasn't.

I moved to at least hug him but he backed further against his door.

"Please don't," he begged.

I moved away and opened my own door. I got out of the car. As I went to close the door I said "Gus?"

"What?"

"What were you going to ask me on Friday night, as we pulled into the driveway?"

"It doesn't matter now," he grumbled.

"Please?" I asked, sounding pitiful and not caring if I did.

"I was going to ask you to marry me," he said in a whisper, then started the engine before I could say anything else. He drove away. I trudged slowly back down the lane through the snow.

⌘⌘⌘⌘⌘

Nothing had ever hurt like this. Both parts of my life were a shambles. Unfortunately, it looked like the only one I could repair was the one I didn't really want. Maybe it didn't matter what I wanted. Gus was right. If I wasn't willing to fight for those things, I didn't deserve to have them. I didn't even know how to fight for what I'd wanted. I never had. Maybe I'd have to make do.

On Sunday night, Paul called to ask if I'd broken things off with Gus.

"Actually, he broke things off with me," I told him bitterly.

"Even better," he said. I wouldn't have thought Paul had it in him to gloat. It was just one more thing I'd been wrong about. On Monday, I called Liberty News to tell them I wouldn't be able to come in anymore. I cowardly avoided talking to both Mike and Richard. I left a message with gum-snapping, Candy. I told my parents that secretarial school had finished early. My heart was broken. It seemed like maybe the best way to deal with that, would be to try not to feel anything at all.

Rosemary showed up at my house on Tuesday.

"Paul told me some of what happened," she confided. "I hope you're not mad at me for knowing about it."

"You should be mad at me. I should have told you all about everything in the first place," I apologized.

"I don't think Paul was very nice to you," she observed.

"In our own ways, I guess we weren't very nice to each other," I said.

"Look," she said "I always thought you'd marry Paul and we'd be like sisters. But maybe you and Paul just grew apart. He seems to care an awful lot about politics now," she mused. "If you really love this other guy, maybe you should be with him instead."

I hugged her. She didn't lie. She didn't manipulate people. She could never have had a secret life. She was just Rosemary and everything she thought and felt was just all out there.

"I don't think I can be with him," I said. "Some things are just too broken to fix."

I moped through the rest of the week. I started to think about the First Lady. I'd always admired President Kennedy but I'd never given much of a thought to his wife, Jackie. She had always seemed to be just about fashion and style. All the bored socialite girls wanted to dress and wear their hair just like her. Now, I started to think of her as a person.

Did she really appreciate being dragged everywhere with the President? Always having to smile and be gracious? Having her family put on display? When I married Paul, this is what I would become, albeit on a much smaller scale. I wondered now, if the First Lady had hopes and dreams of her own. Had she squashed them or put them aside to be with the President?

Pondering the first lady really served no purpose. After all, I didn't know her and it was unlikely that I ever would know her. But thinking about troubles she may have had kept me from thinking about my own. I didn't want to think about those at all. It was just too painful.

I did actually consider joining the Peace Corps like Gus had suggested. It was very tempting to think of leaving all my problems several thousand miles away. It didn't seem right though. Even though I'd been dreaming about it for months, it seemed less like fulfilling a dream and more like just running away at this point. If my fundamental problem was, that I wasn't standing up for myself, and Gus was probably right about that, then running away wasn't going to fix that problem.

On Friday morning, the house phone rang. Gus had been the only person who'd had the number of the phone I'd had installed in my bedroom. That one hadn't rung in a week. It felt like a physical blow to think it might never ring again. I'd probably just have it disconnected eventually. I didn't know if I would be able to. Maybe I'd leave it connected forever and just keep hoping it might ring someday.

I figured the call would be someone for one of my parents or from Paul or Rosemary but the voice on the other end surprised me. It was Richard Noseworthy.

He sounded flustered and annoyed, so I almost didn't recognize him. Flustered and annoyed was more of Mike Flanagan's thing.

"Where are you?" he demanded.

"Well, I'm at home. You called me here, right?" I wasn't even sure how Liberty News had my number. They must have gotten it from the secretarial school when I first started the internship.

"Yeah, obviously, but why aren't you *here*? Candy couldn't get it straight. She said you were sick but she also said you weren't ever coming back."

"Well, I wasn't going to come back," I said.

"What? That makes no sense. Promise to explain it to me sometime. Right now, you've got to get in here. I've been running the paper by myself, all week. I could use your help."

"Where's Mike?' I asked.

"He's back in the hospital. He's much sicker this time. His doctors aren't certain if it's pneumonia again or something worse," he said ominously. "Look, if you come in you can help me and we can go see him and you can tell my why you haven't been here in days. Please, will you come?" He sounded scared and that scared me.

'Yes, I'll come. I'll have to borrow a car."

"Do what you have to," Richard said, "Just get here."

⌘⌘⌘⌘⌘

I called my father at work and asked to borrow the Buick.

"What's wrong with your car, Eleanor?" he asked.

"It's not running, at the moment. I have to get it to the garage later. But right now, I have to go into the city. Someone I met through secretarial school is ill." That was more or less the truth.

"All right. Just be careful where you park the Buick. We can talk about your disaster of a car later.'

I felt hysterical laughter bubble up inside of me and I hung the phone up quickly. If only my father knew that my battered Nash was actually the smallest disaster in my life right at that moment.

⌘⌘⌘⌘⌘

Liberty News had always simmered with a sort of controlled chaos. Mike Flanagan had managed to reign in that chaos. He left just enough of it to fuel creativity and spontaneity. Now, that chaos had been unleashed. Unfettered, it was just chaos; it actually impeded creativity.

Wastepaper baskets overflowed. A couple of them were actually overturned. My former desk looked like a paper bomb had gone off. There was no sign of Candy. A phone rang and nobody answered it. Richard sat in the middle of Mike's glass-walled office looking aggrieved.

"Jeez, Eleanor," he said when I walked in. "Where have you been? I've got every reporter we have out on stories. Your Helpful Harriet replacement quit in a huff two days ago. I don't even know what her issue was…not that she was all that useful anyway. The coffee is three days old. What's this nonsense about you not being able to come in anymore? You're not sick too are you?"

"No," I said "I'm not sick. But why do you need me? Liberty

News has real reporters…"

"What," Richard asked, "Are you talking about? You *are* a real reporter. Your stories are good and Mike's been in a better mood since you started, than I've seen him in all the time I've worked here. You do a lot around here. We *appreciate* you. I thought you liked working here." He looked hurt.

Despite Mike wanting to hire me in the first place, despite praise about my writing when I'd earned it (and constructive criticism when I hadn't) and despite Richard dropping everything, any time I had a question, I hadn't really thought I'd made any difference at Liberty News. When Paul had told me to quit, I'd felt desperately sad about it but it had never occurred to me that there might be sadness on the other end too. I hadn't thought I'd been valued or would be missed.

This was entirely my fault, I realized. They'd always valued me; I just hadn't been able to see the value in myself. Maybe, this was what Gus was telling me. I'd built a life I loved but I'd been willing to let it all go because I hadn't been able to see that what I wanted actually mattered. I'd been selfish then not selfish enough.

Richard was still looking at me with a hurt expression, waiting for me to say something. Why was it my brain never processed the right answer fast enough?

"I'm sorry," I said. "I just…I don't…I…oh bloody hell!" I swore.

Richard burst out laughing.

"Who are you?" he asked, still laughing. "You never curse. Ever. What is wrong with you?" he asked but he was still laughing.

"I honestly don't know," I said, laughing too. It felt good to laugh. I hadn't done it since we'd won the bowling championship a week before. The memory of that helped me focus a little and get more serious.

"I can't even put what's wrong with me into words but I'm working on it and I'm here now," I said. "I don't *like* working here, I *love* working here," I added, surprising myself. It felt nice to be able to say it out loud.

"Well good," Richard said. "While you're trying to figure out your issues, could you help me with mine? Will you type some copy for me and make us some drinkable coffee? Please?"

"Yeah. Yeah, I will," I said.

⌘⌘⌘⌘⌘

Several hours later, we'd restored some order and put the paper to bed. It would come out on Saturday morning like it was supposed to.

Richard said, "You know, I love the writing part of all this and I'm flattered by Mike's faith in me but I'm not sure I'm so great at this running the paper stuff. That's really Mike's gig," he sighed. "Although Mike is great at the writing too. Anyway, I appreciate your help."

"Mike really is the heart and soul of this paper isn't he?" I asked it as a question but I knew the answer. I'd worked here for months now. I'd remembered Mrs. Alvarez the seamstress talking about how Liberty News was really Mike's only love.

"He is," Richard agreed. "So, he'd best be getting better, goddamned soon." He sounded so much like Mike that we both burst out laughing.

⌘⌘⌘⌘⌘

It was late when I got home but my parents were still up.

"No trouble with the Buick?" my father asked.

"None at all. Thank-you for letting me borrow it. Are you and mother going to bed right away or do you have a few minutes?" I asked. "I'd like to talk to you both about something."

Something had shifted inside me after I'd gone to Liberty News to help Richard. Why didn't I deserve a life I wanted? Why couldn't I have a life I'd created for myself? Gus had been right about not standing up for myself. I never had really. I had done things my parents hadn't approved of when I was younger but then, I'd always gone back and tried to be the daughter I thought they wanted.

I didn't feel I needed to rebel just for rebellion's sake as some of my school classmates had. But what I wanted and what they wanted were at odds. I was still young. The decisions I made now would affect the rest of my life. It was probably too late to get Gus back but that didn't mean I had to marry Paul. I hoped my parents would agree to talking right then. If I had too long to think it over, I might not say what I needed to.

"We're listening," my father said. "What's on your mind?"

When I had told Paul the story of everything that had happened since the summer, I'd left out a few things. I hadn't told him about the Peace Corps thing because I felt it wouldn't serve any purpose . He would have said it was silly and that was that. I didn't tell him about Christmas with Gus. I was still somehow trying to not hurt his feelings. Plus, I felt I needed to keep a few details for myself. If memories were all I was going to have then a few of them at least should be private I'd figured.

I felt a little different with my parents. I didn't know if I could make them understand my feelings but I felt if I could, maybe they'd understand my actions.

"I've lied to you and I'm sorry," I said, then I told them everything. To their credit, they listened. At one point my mother said "Really, Eleanor," just as I'd heard her say in my head for a lot of my life. My father asked her to let me finish what I had to say.

My mother spoke first, after I'd finished. My father stayed quiet initially. He seemed to be processing everything I'd said.

"So you're not going to marry Paul?' she asked "You're going to marry this Gus person?"

"I'm not sure I can fix things with Gus," I admitted. It hurt to say it. I was being honest now, though. In for a penny in for a pound, right?

"But," I said, "No. Either way, I'm not going to marry Paul. I'm not going to quit my job either. If you feel you have to ask me to live somewhere else, then go ahead." These were bold word from a woman who didn't have any place to go. But I was feeling bold. Surely I could figure everything else out.

"No one has asked you to live anywhere else," my father said calmly. "However, nobody likes to be lied to," he continued, "and your mother and I are no exception."

"I am sorry," I repeated, feeling slightly less bold.

"What ever will we say to Paul's parents?" my mother lamented.

"It doesn't matter," my father said. "This is really between Eleanor and Paul. They'll work it out between them or they won't. They are adults now, you know."

I couldn't believe what an ally I had in my father. It was a different way for him to behave but then I was behaving differently as well. If I had been standing up for myself from the start, would he have always been so supportive? It was possible. I could have saved myself a lot of heartbreak, maybe. But you can't fix the past, only the present.

"If only you'd agreed to have a debutante's ball," my mother tried again. For her, everything would have been fine if I just hadn't been so stubborn

"It wouldn't have made any difference," I told her gently. I was trying hard not to hurt her feelings. "I'm not like you or Rosemary," I told her. "I respect you both," I added, "but I'm just not wired that way and you know it. You've probably known it since I fell out of that tree and broke my arm. I'm sorry it makes you unhappy but it's just who I am."

My father tried to give me a stern look but I could swear I saw a twinkle in his eye.

"Aside from the lying," he told my mother, "which we didn't appreciate," he reminded me, "All she's really done is work hard and fall in love. She wasn't carousing. She's not pregnant…You're not pregnant are you?" he asked me suddenly.

"No, I am definitely not pregnant," I confirmed.

"Well then…" my father said, then trailed off as if that summed it up.

I couldn't believe how the entire conversation had gone. I realized that unless a lion was chasing you or your walls were literally collapsing, being afraid, was pretty stupid. It just didn't serve a purpose. You couldn't control what other people did or said. You could only control what you did. I'd just learned that sometimes your expectations of how people would react were so far off the mark as to be ridiculous.

I hugged both of my parents. They both reacted with surprise but they both hugged me back.

"Eleanor," my father said as I turned to leave.

"Yes?" I asked.

"I like Paul. I respect how hard he works but I can't say I've been thrilled with his father's plan to turn him into a politician. It's turned him into a bit of a boor."

"I thought so too," I said with a huge smile. For the first time ever, I thought maybe my family wasn't such a bad fit for me after all.

⌘⌘⌘⌘⌘

The next day, I had to make two phone calls. First, I called Paul and asked him to come over.

"I have some work to do," he said.

"It's actually kind of important," I insisted.

He came over grouchy. What I had to tell him wasn't going to improve his mood. He used to be so easygoing. I felt like his political goals were dragging him down. I wondered how much of them were legitimately his and how much they belonged to his father. Unfortunately, I wasn't going to be able to help him figure any of that out.

"Look," Paul grumbled, "if this is about wedding plans, I'd be just as happy to let you deal with everything. I still have a lot of work to do with my career."

"Well," I admitted "It's sort of about wedding plans but you should be happy. You'll have plenty of time to work on your career because there isn't gong to be any wedding."

"Because of some mechanic you met at a bowling alley?" he asked with sarcasm.

"No," I said "Because of me. Because I don't want to marry you. You never even actually asked me. You just assumed we'd get married but I don't want to."

"It doesn't matter what you think," he said. "Your parents…"

I interrupted him. "My parents support me," I said. It felt wonderful to be able to say it. "And it does matter what I think. It just took me a long time to realize it."

"Fine. Do whatever you want. I won't be responsible for your poor choices. anymore" he said angrily.

"You never were," I reminded him as he stomped out.

My second phone call was to Maryann. I was thankful it was a Saturday and Gus would be at work all day. It was really her I needed to talk to anyway. Gus and his mom were close. Unlike me, I don't think he'd ever lied to his parents. I was sure she knew about what had happened between us, even if she didn't know all the details. She sounded surprised to hear from me but she let me talk.

"Remember when you told me I couldn't live in two worlds?"

"Yes," she said.

"Well you were right and I've made my choice. I was kind of a huge jerk," I admitted. "I don't know if I'm going to be able to make things right but I'm going to try. I need your help."

"I'm listening," she said. I told her my plan.

⌘⌘⌘⌘⌘

Mike Flanagan was released from the hospital a second time. His doctors decided it hadn't been anything more serious than pneumonia after all. I thought pneumonia was plenty serious enough.

The second bout with being ill finally made him decide to quit smoking and drinking. He said, "I had to quite drinking and smoking so I could stay alive to run this goddamned newspaper." No one took any offense to this. Richard and the other reporters only wanted to report anyway. Nobody else wanted to run Liberty News. We were all just happy to have Mike back no matter how much complaining he did.

And he did complain. He was beyond cranky, for weeks. I made a lot of coffee. He upped his daily quota of swearing which was saying something for him. He also got Liberty News back under control and he was clearly thrilled to be there even with out nicotine or alcohol.

I talked him into hiring Dawn to replace Candy as Helpful Harriet. She turned out to be really good at the job. Maybe, some of Mike's instincts about people's talents had begun to rub off on me. Richard's daughters finally started to sleep through the night and I got to see him for the first time without dark circles under his eyes.

⌘⌘⌘⌘⌘

The leagues at the Bowl-O-Drome began again, at the end of February, a month or so after the January championship game. I hadn't talked to Gus at all during that time. I had desperately wanted to but I knew I had to show him certain things rather than just telling him. Maryann really had final say over the bowling team and she said it was okay if I stayed. I promised her that if Gus couldn't forgive me and my presence made things awkward I'd leave.

I was at the Bowl-O-Drome really early, on the night when leagues were due to start up again. I had gotten the Nash repaired with money I'd earned at the paper. Even though it was functioning again, I'd asked my father to borrow the Buick. I wasn't entirely certain how Gus would react to seeing me again. I knew what outcome I hoped for but what if he was still really mad? The Nash was a distinctive looking car. What if he took one look at in the parking lot and decided to drive the other way and say the heck with the bowling team? I was really nervous.

He saw me right away when he came in but took his time in talking to Eugene and changing into his bowling shoes. It was everything I could do to sit and wait for him to walk over to lane ten.

"I thought you'd be on your way to Africa or someplace by now." I couldn't tell if he actually wished I was or was somewhat happy to see me. I plunged onwards.

"I had some great dreams about the Peace Corps," I said hoping I sounded calmer than I felt. "I might even still go, someday but somebody recently gave me some really good advice."

"Oh yeah?" he said dubiously. "What might that have been?"

I took a deep breath and tried to let it out slowly.

"He said I should stand up for myself and fight for what I want.

There are things I want more than the Peace Corps right now."

"Why are you here?" he asked.

"Because I want to bowl on this team." I paused, to let that sink in. "There's more than that, too. I want to be with you."

He looked really uncomfortable.

"What happens with your fiance and your parents?" he asked. "You can't lie to them forever."

"I'm done with lying to anyone," I said. "I don't have a fiance anymore. My parents know I'm in love with somebody else. They know I'm in love with you."

He still looked uncertain.

I extended my hand like I was introducing myself. In a way, I guess I was. "Hi, I'm Eleanor. You can call me Ellie if you'd like. Nobody ever did before you but it sounded great when you did. I have a job as a reporter and I bowl on a team at the Bowl-O-Drome. My parents don't understand everything I do but we're communicating these days. Everyone thought I was going to marry this guy but I finally told him it wasn't going to work. I love somebody else. I screwed things up with him but I'm going to fix them if he'll let me. All this is truth, Gus. I don't want two secret lives. I want one life with you. I'm willing to stand up for myself."

There wasn't any more I could say or do. I'd already been rambling on like an idiot. At least I was secure in the knowledge that I'd been an honest idiot.

He took my hand and held it in his for a moment. He looked at me like he'd never seen me before.

"At least bowl with me once," I coaxed. "If you really, really hate it, you can quit."

"Okay," he said finally. He was still holding my hand. "Okay."

⌘⌘⌘⌘⌘

Epilogue

September 1962

Gus and I were trying to simultaneously unwrap and pack our wedding presents. We wanted to make sure we opened them all, so we could write thank-you notes. We didn't want to wait while those gifts were in storage for two years. By the time we got back, we wouldn't remember who had given us what. Besides, we thought two years was too long to have to wait for a thank you note. It would probably be considered rude.

It was taking forever. My plan was to unwrap a gift, then write down a description and the giver's name in a notebook. Almost everything was going into storage but there might be a few things we were going to bring with us. Gus kept picking up random items and making up stories about them or making silly comments. Only Gus could make waffle irons and blenders seem funny. I kept dissolving into helpless laughter. Then, he would laugh. Then, I would lose my place and get my piles mixed up and realize that I hadn't written the correct gift giver's name next to the correct gift.

"We have to get this done," I chastised him but I wasn't able to drum up any sternness about it. I was still giggling.

He picked up a set of tongs and opened and closed them like they were an alligator. He waggled his eyebrows like Grouch Marx. "Of course we do," he said in a goofy voice and I couldn't help laughing again.

He had given me a shot with bowling on the team again and a shot with him too. He had proposed in May.

Rosemary had gotten married in June. I sat on her bed, one last time, helping her adjust her veil. She seemed much older to me. I guess we were both finally grownups. It was a heady feeling and a little bit sad too. I couldn't believe how much had changed in just one year. It was amazing to me and yet all that change would have been incomprehensible to me if you'd suggested it to me a year before.

Paul, of course, was at the wedding.

"How are you Eleanor?" he had asked.

"I'm well, thanks and you?" I'd replied.

"Very well thank you," he'd said.

It was all perfectly civilized. As if I hadn't committed a betrayal. As if he hadn't said awful things. As if our entire history had only ever been just as formal and unemotional as this polite bit of conversation. I didn't know what had made him decide to marry me when he was twelve and I was eight. I probably never would, Maybe he didn't know himself.

Rosemary had confided that he had met someone. I imagined she was probably just another bored socialite girl. Apparently, she wanted everything that Paul wanted. Her dreams were his dreams. There's nothing wrong with supporting someone else's dreams. It's a good thing. You only bump into problems if your dreams are at odds with one another or if one person only cares about their dreams. I never stood up for my dreams. In fact, it took me a long time to even acknowledge that I had them. I can't blame Paul entirely for not being supportive.

I'm happy that he's found someone, though. We assumed so much, for so long but you can't build a relationship on assumptions. That's a great way to make each other unhappy.

As soon as I could, I made sure I introduced Gus to my parents. They liked him, actually. I shouldn't really have been surprised. I hadn't given them enough credit. I had spent years feeling like an alien because I was trying to be who they thought I was. I was so terrified they wouldn't accept me. Yet how could they? I hadn't truly accepted myself.

My father is much more flexible than I would have given him credit for. It's been a bit of an adjustment for my mother but she's trying. When Gus and I set a date for our wedding, she wanted to drag me off to some elegant bridal boutique she knew of. Rosemary had gotten her bridal gown there and it was lovely. It had suited her.

But I told my mother I would be going in a different direction. Her mouth hung open a bit when we walked into Maria Alvarez's shop and she gave me a brief look of panic. By the time Mrs. Alvarez had given my mother a cup of tea and taken my measurements, my mother was holding her own She wasn't entirely comfortable. She does love her sameness, after all, but she was trying.

We compromised when it came to the wedding. My mother, of course, wanted an elaborate wedding, in a church, with an incredibly fancy reception. Party planning was her thing. She was really good at it. I was never going to be good at it and that was okay.

It didn't actually harm me in any way to let my mother plan a big fancy wedding and an even fancier reception. It didn't interfere with what made me, me. My "you-ness" as Gus would have told me. But, I told my mother, after the cake was cut and the elegant people Gus and I didn't really even know had gone home, we were going to have a party at the Bowl-O-Drome. Gus and I had asked Eugene about it. He was happy to host it.

It seemed really important to go back to the beginning. We wanted to honor the circumstances that had brought us to where we were. Circumstances that Gus still insisted were 'supposed to be'. Who knew? Maybe he was right and things couldn't have happened for us in any other way than they had. Could events have transpired in an entirely different way and still brought us to this point? Did it even matter? You could only be where you were.

The wedding and that fabulous party at the Bowl-O-Drome had

been two days before. I hadn't thought I could have been any happier than when we left Bowl-O-Dome's parking lot that night. I was wrong.

Gus had said he had a honeymoon surprise for me.

"Do you trust me?" he'd asked, a couple of months before the wedding. "Do you trust me to plan a honeymoon you'll never forget?"

"Sure," I said "I trust you."

He was amazingly closed-lipped about the whole thing. He refused to tell me anything for months. I tried to get him to spill the secret but it didn't happen.

Finally, on our wedding night, he handed me an envelope.

"What's this?" I asked him.

"Our honeymoon and my wedding present to you. Go ahead and open it."

There were two plane tickets to Ghana in the envelope.

"We're going to Africa on our honeymoon/?" I asked excitedly.

"For two years," he said.

"Two years?!" I exclaimed. "How can we possibly take a two year honeymoon?"

"There should be something else in that envelope," he said.

I upended the envelope and a letter fell out. It was from the Peace Corps.

"I sent our applications in a few months ago," he said. "I was really beginning to bite my nails. Our assignments just came in last week. If they hadn't arrived, I wouldn't have had a spectacular honeymoon to give you. We would have had to spend it in the mystery cave."

That made me laugh. We'd gone back to the mystery cave many times since our first date. I never got tired of it. It had become part of the whole fabric of us.

I stopped laughing, suddenly engulfed by worry.

"You have skills as a mechanic," I said, "what did you say I would do?"

"They need people to teach English," he said. "You're a really good writer and you like words, so I thought that would be a good fit for you. It is isn't it?"

Now he looked worried. I'd meant it when I had told Gus that I might still join the Peace Corps. But I had been so caught up with everything else, I hadn't even thought of it in a while. I hadn't dreamed of it in months. Before, I had been almost obsessive about finding out more but I had eased up on that obsession some. I hadn't even occurred to me that what I'd learned at Liberty News could translate to something useful I could do in the Peace Corps.

"It's okay, right? I haven't made the most horrible blunder of our marriage in the first 24 hours, have I?" he asked.

"It's okay," I said enfolding him in a hug that almost knocked him over.

Then I had one more attack of insecurity.

"How come?" I asked him.

"How come what?" he asked.

"How come you wanted to do this? I know you thought the Peace Corps was a good idea in theory. It was one of the reasons I liked you right away. But how come you decided it was a good idea for *you*?"

"It was your dream but you wanted me more. You were willing

to let it go for me. The least I could do is be willing to do it for you."

THE END

Thank-you! Thank-you! Thank-you!

This book was written as part of National Novel Writing Month. As such, many words went onto paper in a fairly short period of time. There were a lot of people who helped me to do that and make being a published author a reality. I hope I don't forget anyone!

To Laura, Dawn, Heather, Naomi, Scott and Cliff for volunteering to edit for me. Thank-you! I know not everybody got a shot at it. That was either due to my impatience to publish (and it was still a much slower process than I'd hoped) or my terror at the thought of six simultaneous edits! However, I'm still incredibly grateful to everyone who offered. The suggestions I did get were awesome. Any failure in the editing process is mine alone.

Thanks to Philip, my friend at work, who promised to harass me, daily, throughout the month of November, and did.

To all my family and friends new and old, in person and on Facebook, who said encouraging things, who commented on excerpts I posted, who asked how it was going and who said you couldn't wait to read it, thank-you! All those comments and feedback kept me going. I hope you're not disappointed. I have wonderful, supportive people in my life and I am blessed.

Thank-you, Zach, for faithfully asking me about my word counts, every single day and taking my picture for the back cover.

Thank-you, Nathaniel for designing my front cover. (And to my mom for helping me tweak it when the formatting was wrong.)

Thank-you, Jeff, for bringing me Creamsicles while I wrote. They were way more inspirational than you know. Thanks for calling me "writer girl" which made me feel much cooler than I probably am. Thanks for always supporting me and loving me and generally putting up with me for almost a quarter of a century.

36481898R00095

Made in the USA
Lexington, KY
21 October 2014